A
HARLEQUIN
Book

1312

PEPPERCORN HARVEST

by

IVY FERRARI

HARLEQUIN BOOKS
WINNIPEG • CANADA

First published in 1968 by Mills & Boon Limited,
50 Grafton Way, Fitzroy Square, London, England.

SBN 373-01312-4

Harlequin Canadian edition published June, 1969
Harlequin U.S. edition published September, 1969

All the characters in this book have no existence outside the imagination of the Author, and have no relation whatsoever to anyone bearing the same name or names. They are not even distantly inspired by any individual known or unknown to the Author, and all the incidents are pure invention.

Printed in Canada

1312

CHAPTER ONE

On the London Underground, Bakerloo line, the muggy spring evening seemed stifling. Sitting between two portly business men, Grace Haydon glimpsed a headline on a newspaper.

'Snow Again In The North.'

She closed her eyes, seeing again the snow-capped Cheviot Hills brooding above the rolling vale that was home. Spring came so late to Northumberland.

A wave of violent homesickness assailed her. She could almost smell the sharp sweetness of the moorland air. Then her eyes opened again to the sight of swaying, weary-faced commuters. For nearly eighteen months now she had been one of them, self-condemned to a drab, meaningless routine.

At first London had meant escape, a flight from pain and tragedy, but from the first she had fought against totally committing herself. Attaching herself to a typing agency, she had taken only jobs of a temporary nature, avoiding permanent loyalties and relationships. She had even moved flats three times before finding a flatmate who treated her with the casual indifference she sought. Secretly she had always known homesickness would win in the end.

These last months it had been stronger even than the bitter memories she had left in the north. She had struggled against the urge to go home, knowing she would surely find old pain and new disillusionment. And now—

'Now I can go,' the thought came. 'It's not my

decision any longer. Alec needs me.'

She fingered the letter in her handbag, but already she had memorized its curt sentences. Her brother, Doctor Alec Haydon, was a man of few words.

'I've got bad news, Grace. Isobel has gone down with T.B. and has to be in hospital for six months. You can guess just what a blow this is. She is worrying herself sick over Simon and hoping, as I am, that you will help us out. You know I wouldn't dream of asking you to come back except in an emergency like this, but we need you desperately, both to look after Simon and take over Isobel's surgery work – your old job, in fact.'

Alec had gone on to say that his wife was to be admitted to hospital in a few days and that on the following Friday he was due in London for a medical conference. 'I will call at your flat Friday evening,' he finished. 'This will give you a few days to think things over. If you do decide to come I hope you can arrange to travel back with me on the Saturday morning.'

A rather pathetic postscript ended the page. 'If it's "No" I shan't blame you, though heaven knows what I shall do.'

Tears stung her eyes. The train rocked and swayed on its way to the northern suburbs. Well, what *would* he do? Simon was only eight years old, and Isobel, besides being loving wife and mother, had coped cheerfully with surgery records, with correspondence and the endless telephone calls; all the work Grace herself had once done. Alec had found it impossible to get a suitable substitute. The surgery at Lintlaw House, in the village of Abbotshaws, was too isolated to attract applicants.

Now Isobel's collapse brought strong sensations of guilt. 'But I couldn't have stayed – I couldn't,' she told herself. And again the chill shadow of that old tragedy moved over her, so that a shiver came. To go back now, to relive it all again, to have people talk of Douglas – she had no illusion as to the outcome. Once she returned the past eighteen months would fade as if they had never been. The old pain would be there, waiting, the old resentment and helpless searing anger....

Yet she was drawn achingly towards home, sick for a sight of Whittingham Vale, a rolling green offshoot of Coquetdale, with the flat-headed Simonside Hills brooding on the skyline, and further north the hump-backed range of the Cheviots. In the vale she had been born and reared, had fallen in love, known her deepest emotions.

Douglas was dead, she told herself. But Alec was very much alive. She owed him sisterly help and loyalty. Little Simon needed her and Isobel deserved peace of mind, reassurance about her child. Alec was right when he wrote: 'Heaven knows what I'll do'. Their parents were elderly and retired to Bournemouth, for their mother had been Hampshire-born. There could be no question of disrupting *their* lives.

And today was Friday. Tonight she would see Alec, they would talk. But already in her heart she knew what she must do.

At Swiss Cottage she was borne out on the home-going stream, climbed the escalator to the roar of the Finchley Road traffic. She ran against the sullen drizzle, her slim shoulders hunched, her red-gold hair in damp tendrils about her face. Fellows Road, a turn left and left again and she entered a Victorian house divided into flats. Groping for her key on the way up-stairs, she almost fell over a man sitting on the top step.

'Oops, sorry! . . . Alec!'

No one could have mistaken them for anything but brother and sister. Standing, Alec revealed a tall muscular body, darker auburn hair, but blunt freckled features instead of her fine-boned delicacy. Their eyes were of an identical smoky blue.

'You got my letter, Gay?' he asked.

'Yes, Alec.' She reached out, touched him blindly on the arm. Gay was his pet name for her. 'Been waiting long?' Her voice was unsteady.

He reached for a sheepskin-lined jacket dumped on the doorstep. 'Just about half an hour . . . I came dressed for the Antarctic and find London stewing in fug. I can't think how you stand it!'

His light tone did not deceive her. The door shut, they faced each other in the comfortable living room of her shared flat.

'Is your flat-mate due in?'

'No. Brenda's gone to a works survey with her boss – in Manchester. We're all alone.'

'Good. Make me a cup of tea, Gay. We can worry about eating later.'

She switched on the kettle in the kitchenette, then handed him a cigarette. 'Oh, I forgot – it's a pipe now, isn't it?'

He brought one out of his pocket, gazed fixedly at the empty bowl. She spoke hurriedly: 'Alec, I'm so sorry. Just how bad is she?'

'Bad enough. She's in the Chest Block at Tynehill General. It'll be at least a six months' job.'

'Are both lungs affected, then?'

He threw himself into an armchair, crammed the pipe absent-mindedly back in his pocket. 'There's a patch on one, pitting on the other.'

'But Isobel was always so healthy.'

'She was. But strain and overwork, plus a bad go of 'flu. . . . You know as well as I do it can and does happen.'

'You mean – since I left—'

He shook his head. 'Not altogether a clear case of cause and effect, so don't look so guilty. There *were* other reasons. I wrote you about taking over old Doctor Peters' patients, didn't I? True, I got a new partner to help me, Martin Finch. But there was no extra help for Isobel on the surgery side. You remember Agnes gave notice about that time? We haven't been able to get a living-in housekeeper since.'

He went on talking as Grace set cups on a tray. 'Isobel got 'flu when we had the February epidemic, and afterwards it was just a downward spiral – no appetite, a cough, loss of weight. Then the tests. . . . Thank heaven for the new T.B. drugs. At least we can be sure of her recovery. But it was no end of a blow.'

Grace made tea and carried in the tray. 'How is Simon taking it?'

'He's a bit forlorn and neglected, as you can imagine. And it doesn't help that they won't allow child visiting on T.B. wards. Rightly so, of course.'

She poured his tea. An awkward silence fell. At last she said gently: 'You did right to ask me, Alec.'

His head came up eagerly, but the uncertainty still in her eyes made him hesitate. 'You always said the work you were doing down here wasn't all that important, Gay.'

'It isn't. You know I didn't come to London seeking a career. It's just – a job.'

His face was troubled as he said: 'You might as

well add – "That's not quite the point, is it?" '

She walked to the window, leaving her tea untouched. The rain fell fine and straight, darkening the pavements and the sooty front gardens, washing a bed of dusty crocuses. Alec's voice came quietly: 'It's nearly eighteen months ago now, Gay.'

Again his use of the family nickname touched her. She saw them as children, running on the moors above Abbotshaws, free as the curlews beating over the vale.

'I know,' she said.

'I thought you came to London to forget. Didn't it work?'

She shook her head. 'I don't know. Perhaps it did – just a little. And now you're asking me – to come back.' She hurried on. 'I do want to help you, Alec. More than anything. If only—'

'If only we didn't live a few miles from Goatshiels?'

She winced at the name.

He pressed: 'Wouldn't it help to talk about it now? At the time you wouldn't. You pulled that pale cold shutter down over your face. None of us could get near you or help you.'

She was silent, holding her slim body tense. He said casually: 'Would there be another cup of tea?'

'Sorry, Alec. I'm neglecting you.' She re-filled his cup.

'Now get rid of that cold brew of yours and have a fresh cup.' She recognized his surgery voice. 'Then come and sit down.'

When she had obeyed he said: 'Gay, I hate to see you like this – still lonely and bitter.'

'I have been lonely, yes. But even loneliness was better than pity – better than everyone in Abbotshaws gossiping—'

Alec shook his head. 'What happened at the High Stones of Goatshiels is still vivid in your mind, I know. But in the village it was a nine days' wonder. Life goes on, you know. When Ellis Ridley disappeared after the funeral—'

He broke off as he saw the fear and loathing in her face.

'I'll never forgive Ellis Ridley as long as I live!' she flashed.

His face hardened. 'That's wrong, Gay – and you know it. Ellis wasn't responsible for his brother's death, whatever *you* choose to think. Negligent, perhaps.'

She turned on him in anger. 'What he did was a crime to me. If he hadn't been so set on his own selfish pleasure, Douglas might have been alive today.'

Alec rested his elbows on his knees, stared at his linked hands. 'No one knows what really happened. There were very few facts to go on, after all.'

'Enough for me, though. Douglas fell from the rocks in the mist. He'd obviously walked too near the edge. *You* know that path over the High Stones – it narrows to a razor's edge in parts. He was in bad shape, it's true – when Sandy Currie found him. But you said yourself at the inquest he might have been saved but for the long exposure to rain and cold.'

She went on as if reciting a well-known lesson. 'Sandy ran straight to Peppercorn for Ellis, but he couldn't make anyone hear. The doors were locked. There were lights, music being played. Jess Robson, the housekeeper, was staying the night in the village. . . . Sandy said he made enough noise to wake the dead, that no one inside could help hearing him. But no one came. In the end he had to go right over to Lordhope for help – help that was too late. That night Douglas died in hospital.'

'Don't go on, Gay – tearing yourself to pieces all over again. What good does it do now?'

She ignored him. 'When Sandy passed near Peppercorn just after dawn, seeing to his sheep, he saw a girl leave the house. She'd been there all night, of course. That was why even the hospital hadn't had a reply to their phone calls. Ellis Ridley was too busy with his latest conquest.'

'It was a human enough reason, Gay. Not that I approve, but that part of it is purely his affair.'

'Local opinion didn't think so. And he made no attempt to answer any criticism. All he did was run away as soon as the funeral was over – heaven knows where.'

Alec sighed and stirred. 'Then you'll be glad to hear he may never come back at all. Peppercorn is let on a furnished lease to some people called MacEwan. They've been there nearly a year now.' He went on gently: 'I promise you, Gay, if you come back you'll be too busy to go anywhere near Goatshiels. And people will be tactful. They won't rake up the past.'

After hesitating he continued on a firmer note: 'I won't beat about the bush. I need you desperately, and so does Simon.'

'I know.' She managed a misty smile. 'I can't refuse you, Alec.'

His face cleared. He got up and hugged her. 'I hope you'll never regret it, Gay. . . . We've all missed you so.'

'I've missed you too. But I thought London might hold some miracle cure to set me free of – all that happened.'

'Maybe you were looking in the wrong place. The cure could be back home all the time.' He patted her shoulder. 'Sometimes we have to face our nightmares before we can overcome them.'

She moved away impatiently. 'Don't, Alec. I don't want to talk about the past any more.'

He nodded. 'All right, then. We'll talk of practical issues. What about your job – this flat?'

She turned to face him. 'I've just finished a fortnight's work. I've already rung the agency to ask them not to book me into another job until I contact them. They'll keep me on their books for a while, and then if I *don't* come back after a few months they'll just write me off.'

'And the flat?'

'That's no problem either. Brenda has a friend who is desperate for cheaper accommodation. She'll move in like a shot if I go. My rent's paid up to the end of the month. All I have to do is to leave a note for Brenda.'

Alec looked about him curiously. 'Haven't you any gear to move – any bits and pieces of your own?'

She smiled, shaking her head. 'Just a few books and my clothes. I've never had the home-making urge here. It's just been four walls and a roof.'

He looked relieved. 'You mean you'll come with me in the morning?'

She quoted softly: ' "If t'were done . . . t'were well it were done quickly—" ' She glanced at the clock. 'Give me ten minutes to change, then we'll go somewhere and eat. You'll have to bring me up to date with all the village gossip!'

'Bless you, Gay,' was all he said. But his eyes spoke volumes.

Next morning Alec drove steadily up the A.1,

Grace at his side. For almost an hour they had been silent. Absorbed in her thoughts, she was almost oblivious of the passing traffic. Only the direction held meaning for her, as they advanced through the Midlands, towards that first outpost of the real north, Scotch Corner.

She was remembering her childhood in the family home of Grey Gables, on the outskirts of Abbotshaws; incidents she had shared with Alec; building the aerial railway from the barn to the attic window, rescuing a wounded owl from the stable roof, crying over old Tess the collie, found dead in her kennel after a night of storm. There had been other pets, too, from ponies to guinea-pigs.

Later she spent four years at boarding school near Durham, years of continued homesickness which remained her own grievous secret. Her reticent nature found it easier to bear trouble than communicate it to others. Somehow she had stuck it out until she was seventeen, when she came joyfully to work for Alec, now newly qualified as a doctor and opening his surgery at Lintlaw House.

It was a humble enough career, but she was more than content to interest herself in the health and concerns of the villagers, their joys and sorrows. She found a dear friend in Isobel and became an adoring aunt to young Simon. Then, when her parents retired, she moved into Lintlaw House altogether.

At nineteen she was flirting in a casual way with young farmer admirers. Then at a dance she met Douglas Ridley and her gentle, carefree world was turned upside down.

The Ridley half-brothers shared the isolated homestead of Peppercorn, near the head of Coquetdale, a lonely desolate region where leaping hill streams converged on the narrow upper reaches of the Coquet river. The house had once been a shooting-box, a sturdy rambling stone building in an acre of garden and hilly pasture. Like all lonely dwellings it had a lost, dreamlike quality, a suggestion of sorcery, of mystic communion with the clouded summits. Walking the grey London streets she had often wondered if Peppercorn really existed. Only three hundred odd miles away, it could have belonged to another planet, so far removed was it from the ceaseless fret of the modern world.

Douglas Ridley, the younger brother, was a local land-agent and auctioneer, whose activities spread far into the Scottish borders. He was vigorous, ambitious, with a gay, bold charm which opened all doors for him. Local girls pursued him, but it was Grace who got the proposal and the ring. Then began for her a time of rapture and deep happiness. The summer of her engagement held days of hazy heat, when the hills shimmered in a pearly haze. They rode the hill tracks, Grace on Douglas's winsome mare, Black Bess, Douglas on one of his brother's hunters; they lazed for hours beside rocky outcrops, under the fiery blaze of the gorse, or fished the bright glancing burns, tumbling ice-cold from the summits. Day of happiness followed day, their love mounting to its climax of marriage. She could see no fault in Douglas and marvelled daily that he should love her, who was so shy and ordinary.

Of Ellis Ridley she knew little and shrank from knowing more. In the district he had a strange, rather sinister reputation. He was six years older than Douglas, who was then twenty-six, and had a fatalistic driving restlessness which took him for months, sometimes years, from his home at Peppercorn. Local farmers eyed him askance, spoke of his dead Welsh mother as a 'foreigner', accused him of scandalous adventures which lost nothing in the telling. He had run a private air-line in Canada, a breeding stud in Ireland, and dabbled in real estate on the Costa Brava. His sudden swooping returns to Peppercorn disconcerted the plain-living, long-settled dalesmen.

'Aye, Ah see he's back! What's he been up to this time, I wonder?' one shepherd would ask another in the Ram Inn.

'Very like some lass got her claws into him in foreign parts – and he's run for shelter!' would be the ironic rejoinder.

She had met Ellis Ridley for the first time at her engagement party at Grey Gables, just before her parents' retirement. He arrived late and stood in the doorway surveying the guests, a tall man with a craggy, imperious face which might have been handsome but for the white scar over one temple. Grace tensed with shock at sight of him. He was like Douglas and yet so unlike, cast in a similar pattern but from a darker flawed mould.

Douglas introduced him. He held her hand for a disconcerting length of time, giving her a measured scrutiny. Then he smiled. 'So you're Grace.' He turned to Douglas. 'Where did you find her – at Brinkburn?'

'Brinkburn?'

'Surely you remember the legend that there were once fairies there?' He held Grace's eyes again. She saw now that where those of Douglas were blue, his were a stormy grey, holding a depth of meaning she could not fathom. 'So you're to be the bride of Peppercorn,' he went on. 'You know the old verse, of course?' And he chanted softly:

' "Tell him to buy me an acre of land,
Parsley, Sage, Rosemary and Thyme;
And sow it all over with one peppercorn,
For once he was a true love of mine."

I hope your own prospect is less bleak.'

A shiver troubled her, a haunting presage, she now knew, of the tragedy waiting only weeks away. She collected herself and said coolly:

'Yes, I know the Ballad of Whittingham Fair. Was that really how the house got its name?'

'So the tale goes.'

'It was good of you to agree that we should live there. I think it's a wonderful old place.'

'I'm glad you like it. And as I am away so much it seems the obvious arrangement. You will, I hope, keep a bedroom for the lone wanderer, though?'

'It is half your house, isn't it?' she said quietly.

'Possessions mean very little to me.' His eyes held a tinge of irony. 'If I'd been as lucky as Douglas, finding a red-haired fairy on my doorstep, I might have wanted to settle down, too.'

She blushed, made an excuse to speak to another guest. Under that disconcerting stare she felt like a butterfly pinned down for inspection. Yet many times that evening, when Douglas was talking to others, she found herself watching Ellis. That dark, scarred face, so steely and self-possessed, was occasionally shadowed by another element, whether of cynicism, despair or even loneliness she could not guess. She wondered about the scar and thought him a romantic if rather frightening figure, a fitting master for the lonely house among the hills.

She noticed too that he drew the women with careless ease. One girl she knew scarcely left his side, blonde Angela Forster, daughter of a local gentleman farmer. Angela had dabbled in a modelling course, but was then relaxing in moneyed leisure at home. She was using every wile of her training, presenting her tended beauty at a dozen alluring angles. And though Ellis Ridley gave her his amused attention, to Grace it seemed that the veiled irony was still there. . . .

She opened her eyes with a start, to find the car well past Scotch Corner and switchbacking over the rolling Durham fells. There was a sense now of space and light and distance. She rolled down the window, sniffed the soft bleak air.

'Ah, that's better!'

'I thought you were asleep.'

'No, just dozing. Alec, would you like me to drive for a spell? I renewed my licence recently, so I could drive out of London at week-ends in a hire car. I promise you I'm not rusty.'

'No, thanks all the same, Gay. I like to drive my own car – you'd find me a cantankerous passenger.'

They chatted awhile. 'Is Angela Forster married yet?' she asked.

'No. And gossip goes that she's waiting for Ridley to come back.'

'That's unlikely, I hope?' His very name chilled her.

'Most unlikely, as I told you. She *has* shown some interest in young Finch, my partner – though possibly only as a presentable escort.'

'Oh yes, your new partner. What's he like?'

Alec skilfully by-passed a lorry before replying:

'He'll do. I think he came up expecting us all to be wearing skins, though. Couldn't grasp the local lingo, either. It's taken time for the village to accept a Londoner. But Simon took to him from the first.'

They stopped at a roadside café for a snack. Then Alec said thankfully: 'We should see the far side of the Tyne before dark. Try to take another nap as we go, Grace. You look tired.'

She dozed and dreamed fitfully. She was back in Abbotshaws, in the time of her great happiness, the harvest before last. The heather was purple on the high ridges, the cornfields in the vale a bright patchwork among the rolling pastures, blonde barley, golden oats and buff-shadowed wheat. Now she was driving with Douglas up the high reaches of Coquetdale, and on to the rough hill track to Peppercorn. The house stood square to the north, half-way down the hillside, with a dark grove of pines for an eastern windbreak, and facing the bleak ranges of the Cheviot foothills. But in the stone-walled garden above the burn the grass was warm, and late butterflies tangled in a riotous mass of golden rambler roses.

They lay in the sun, holding hands. Douglas gently bit her fingers, then rolled over to look into her face, his eyes warm with longing. 'Peppercorn needs a bride, darling. It's getting dour and crusty, like an old man.'

'I think it's perfect,' she said dreamily. Already she loved every inch of it, the handsome rooms, the big stone-flagged kitchen, the stables and the steep home pasture. She was rather nervous of Jess Robson, the forthright, rather possessive housekeeper, but Jess would not be staying on. They were keeping Billy Middlemass, the quiet devoted odd-job man, who was also gardener and stableman when required.

'It *will* be perfect,' Douglas argued, 'with your face reflected in its mirrors. . . . Oh, but I shall want to show you off. We'll give parties, start entertaining. . . . Until the family comes along, of course. We'll have sons, I think. Two dark like me, then maybe I'll let you have two little girls, with hair like a spun sunset, just like their mother's—'

Grace shivered and sat up. 'Don't, Douglas,' she said faintly. 'You made a goose walk over my grave. Let's not count on too much. Sometimes I'm frightened. We've got so much, everything we ever wanted. I wonder sometimes if it can last. . . .'

'That's why I'm rushing the wedding,' he teased. 'Once we're married we're safe from the bludgeoning of fate.'

'Things can happen after marriage, too,' she warned him.

'Yes, but then we'll be together. No one can come between us.' His smile had gone, and she thought she detected a hint of urgency in his tone.

'I shall still worry after we're married, Douglas. You've got to promise me you won't take so many risks. You know how fast you drive. And riding, too. Going hell for leather at the point-to-point.'

He laughed. 'It's in the Ridley blood, darling. I'm like a cat with nine lives. Douglas Ridley, the man they couldn't kill!'

'If anything happened to you I wouldn't want to go on living. Oh, Douglas, hold me tight. . . .'

That evening he showed her a small grove of rowans beyond the western wall of the pasture. Here were small mounds on the sheep-bitten turf, with carved names on weatherbeaten crosses. A favourite pony, two dogs, several cats and a tame jackdaw – all were buried here. He told her their stories, and came last to a carved cross a little distance away.

'Trixie was a mare who belonged to Ellis. But no one could call *him* sentimental about animals. He schooled her from a filly, but she always had a touch of the devil in her. The truth was she couldn't take his rough handling. In the end she kicked him in the face – marked him for life. He was twelve at the time.'

Her blood chilled, there in the fading light, under the high summits of the hills. She was glad to go back into the paddock again, to feel the warmth of his arm about her. Yet she was impelled to ask more.

'His mother died when he was very young, didn't she?'

'He was four – just old enough to remember. Father married again within the year. History has it that Welsh Myfanwy led him a dance, anyway. She was a wild, untamed piece, juding by the stories I've heard. Used to walk barefoot on the moor in an old cloak. Some of the old folks had it she was a witch. *My* mother was a good solid Northumbrian. She was kinder to Ellis than he deserved, too. He was a shocking problem child. She nearly broke her heart trying to tame him.'

'But in the end he must have resigned himself to a stepmother?' Grace found this old history disturbing.

Douglas shrugged. 'She did her part. But he would never call her Mother. I remember Father beating the daylights out of him because of it.'

'Will Ellis come here often, after we're married?'

'Not if I can help it. He has too much of a reputation where women are concerned.'

They walked round the front of the house and into

the shadowed hall. Douglas pulled her close. 'You know what? I'm sure he's jealous. I saw the way he looked at you.'

'He scares me,' she confessed. 'He's so like you, and yet so different. When I see him I'm reminded of one of those bad dreams, when someone you know begins to turn into a sinister stranger.'

'Don't worry, angel. I won't let him near you. And we'll be married in six weeks. We'll be sharing our dreams then, and they'll all be good ones.'

His kisses drove away her doubts and fears.

'Wake up, Gay. Here's canny Newcastle!'

Alec's voice roused her. She opened her eyes to city lights, to neon signs and a blur of increased traffic. Then ahead she saw the light-spangled span of the New Tyne Bridge, and moments later they had crossed the river into Northumberland.

Tears rushed to her eyes. The transition from past happiness to present pain was too sudden, too cruel. Alec glanced at her, and said in concern:

'I was hoping you wouldn't be too tired to stop at the hospital to see Isobel. It would mean so much to her – to know you've arrived.'

She blinked back her tears. 'Of course, Alec.'

Alec's wife lay flat on her back in a single ward in the Chest Block, so wan and listless Grace knew an intense pity. She masked it with a quick smile and a word of greeting. Isobel's relief at the sight of her was overwhelming.

'I didn't dare hope, Grace,' she said weakly. 'I can start getting better now I know Simon will be well looked after.'

Isobel was a Scot, with dark deep-set eyes and high Celtic cheekbones. Now, with the flesh fallen away, she was a gaunt, sickly shadow of her former self.

Grace held her hand, while Alec went to have a word with the house physician. 'Who has been looking after Simon, then?' she asked.

'Oh, Jess. Usually she only helps part-time, but she's been staying until Simon's bedtime.'

'Jess?'

'Didn't Alec tell you? We got Jess Robson in when Agnes left.'

'He didn't tell me.' Grace tried to hide her disturbance. Jess, from Peppercorn, working now at Lintlaw House – it seemed there was no hope of her ever forgetting the old pain. . . .

She roused herself to say further reassuring words, received a few instructions on Simon's welfare, then Alec came to collect her and say good-bye to his wife. Grace could see how even this short visit had tired her. She pressed Isobel's hand. 'Don't worry about a thing. All you've got to think about now is getting better and coming back to us all,' she said gently.

On the road home, over the darkening moors, Alec himself revived the subject of Jess. 'We were darned lucky to get her. Lucky, too, that you know her. Makes things easier all round.'

Grace was too tired and dispirited to argue. When the car eventually came to rest in the drive of Lintlaw House, darkness had fallen on the vale. She stumbled out, stiff and weary, breathing the bleak spring freshness of the air. An owl hooted softly in the trees behind the church, a familiar sound of home.

In the wide, low-ceilinged hall Jess Robson came forward to greet them, a rosy bustling woman with a crown of sandy hair. She gave Grace a firm handshake.

'Bye. it's good to see you again, Miss Haydon . . .

Aye, I've been helping out, looking after the bit laddie as best I could. You're looking rare and peaky after London. And it's a right long drive. Come away in to the fire and I'll have supper in in two shakes.'

Grace relaxed gratefully by the study fire. Alec excused himself to have a word with his partner. In a moment or two Jess brought a tea-tray.

'You'll want a cup of tea before owt else.' She poured it. 'I saw you got a bit put out, seeing me here. I dare say it brought back things you'd like best to forget. But it suits me well enough, right on my own doorstep, you might say.'

Grace remembered that Jess's father, a retired shepherd, lived in a cottage near the church.

'So you keep house for your father now, Jess?'

'Aye, that's right. He's bedridden with the arthritis, and just sits up all day in his bed by the window, where he can see the hills. His old dog Moss sits with him. He's on his last legs, poor old thing. . . . There's your tea now. I'm glad to see you here, for the bairn's sake, Miss Haydon.'

'And I'm glad you're here, Jess,' Grace felt obliged to say, though with a sinking heart. Jess had always been garrulous and forthright. It was inevitable that she would re-open many old wounds.

Later Jess brought in supper, a light meal of cold ham and salad, then announced that she was going home. Alec entered next in the company of a fair, broadly-built young man.

'Grace, meet Martin Finch, my new partner.'

She shook hands, seeing a cheerful relaxed face, disarming blue eyes. 'I've heard so much about you, Miss Haydon, especially from Simon. We certainly need your help. It was wonderful of you to come.'

Alec announced that Simon was sleeping soundly and that Grace need not worry about him at all until morning. As soon as supper was over she stood up. 'I'm sorry I'm such poor company. Do you mind if I go to bed right away?'

'Best place for you. You look all in. Sleep well, Gay – and don't worry. It'll all work out,' Alec assured her.

Martin Finch jumped up to open the door for her. 'See you tomorrow, Miss Haydon.'

'You'd better start calling me Grace,' she smiled.

His response was eager. 'Then it must be Martin, too.'

'Good night, Martin.' This time there was no mistaking the admiration in his glance. She held her shoulders a little straighter as she left the room, and wondered if she looked a wreck. It was a long time since she had responded to a man's smile.

Grace slept deeply and woke at seven-thirty. From her window she saw the vale through a pearly mist, rising even now to reveal the crags of the opposite ridge. She glimpsed the familiar descending pastures, the dry-stone walls climbing the slopes, and the sturdy dark stone houses under the lofty church tower. Rooks circled in the milky sky and from far and near came the plaintive cries of the Cheviot sheep.

She was home again. Perhaps Alec was right and she had stayed away too long. Here grief would be diluted by home blessings.

She dressed and left her room, eager to see Simon. Then a rusty-haired tornado swept into her arms. She hugged him tight, smiling down into eyes exactly like Alec's.

'Simon! My, how you've grown!' She traced his

adorable snub nose, saw the wide mischievous mouth relax into a grin.

'You've been ages getting up, Auntie Grace. I've been sitting on the stairs, waiting.'

She ruffled his unruly mop. 'When did you get up, then?'

'Seven, of course! I've got to feed my animals before breakfast.' He spoke with growing confidence. She had not missed his first anxiety, the reassurance that she was unchanged now lighting his face. 'I've got two new guinea-pigs since you were here. I call them Nelson and Napoleon. I've got a white rabbit too, called Queenie.'

'Why Queenie?'

'Because Dad once had a rabbit called Queenie. He told me. I've got a jackdaw, too. It hurt its wing and I mended it, and now it won't go away.'

'Hasn't it got a name?'

'No, 'course not!' He explained patiently, 'It's wild, that's why. Wild things don't have names.'

As they went downstairs Grace remembered again Simon's obsession with wild life in all its forms. Living as he did in a part of the country almost untroubled by the harsher aspects of civilization, the haunt of many wild animals and birds able to live their natural lives without undue disturbance, he had spent long, happy hours watching small creatures, listening to the tales of old shepherds and molecatchers, to the country lore of the village boys. Alec had encouraged his interest by buying him the best books on natural history, and for a small boy his knowledge was remarkable.

'I'm glad you've come,' he confided suddenly. 'Mrs. Robson's always telling me to be a good boy –

it gets a bit much, sometimes. It's different if Mummy says it. I wish she wasn't ill, don't you, Auntie Grace? Daddy says it's not serious, she just has to have a long rest in bed. I bet she hates that. Wouldn't you hate it?'

'I expect I should,' she smiled. 'I smell bacon. Who's cooking breakfast?'

'Mrs. Robson – she's in the kitchen. But she said I had to take you straight into the dining-room.' He hesitated. 'We might just have time for a quick look at Nelson and Napoleon.'

'I don't think Mrs. Robson would like that. Breakfast first, don't you think?'

They took their seats at the big round table in the pleasant room to the left of the hall. The tall window, flanked by folded white shutters, overlooked the front lawns with the village street beyond. Simon talked at top speed, about school, the new nests up in the spinney, and lastly his visits to old Will, Jess's father.

'He makes smashing mats, with texts worked in them, all with bits of rag. I told him I'd take you to see them.'

'I can see I'm going to be very busy,' she teased.

Martin Finch came in. 'Good morning, Grace.' He nudged Simon in the ribs. 'Learned to make that knot yet?'

'You bet! I've made it six times. Have you found any nests yet, Doctor Finch?'

'Not a single one. I just haven't got the hang of it. I was sure I spied one last night, but it was just a piece of old knitting someone had thrown in a bush.'

Grace helped Simon to cornflakes. 'What is this – a mutual educational effort?'

Martin laughed. 'You could call it that. I'm teaching him Scout lore, and he's putting me right on the birds and the bees.'

'Doctor Finch is hopeless!' Simon told her. 'He doesn't even know the difference between a crow and a peewit.'

'He'll learn.' Grace turned to Martin. 'You're a Londoner, aren't you?'

'Kensington, to be precise. I fancied a year or two in the wilds.'

'And how do you like it?'

'I wasn't too sure at first.' His gaze was frank and unabashed. 'Now I'm glad I came.'

Jess entered with coffee and bacon. 'Good morning, Miss Haydon. Doctor asked me to get breakfast this morning, as you would be tired. But it would suit me better in future to come later, then I can stay and cook the lunch instead.'

'Certainly, Jess. I'll take over breakfast tomorrow. Then I'll be free for morning surgery while you attend to the house.'

'Aye, that's it.' Jess removed the cereal plates with bold clashing movements. 'You're no' to worry about the domestic side, Miss Haydon. You'll have enough with the bairn and the surgery. And I like to do things my own way.'

Grace bit her lip. Jess was one of the best, but she brooked no interference. She could see difficulties ahead.

When Jess had gone Martin gave her a sympathetic smile. 'You'll tear your hair when you see the muddle we're in – in the surgery, I mean.'

'Oh, I'll soon slip back into the routine.' She handed him his coffee.

'At least you won't have to learn the language first,

as I did. It sounded like Hindustani to me. I can't say the patients have taken to me yet, either. It seems I'm too young, I laugh too much and I'm not married.'

Simon spoke with his mouth full. 'You could marry Auntie Grace. She's quite good about birds, and you could teach her to do knots.'

Martin's eyes brimmed with laughter.

'Manners, Simon!' Grace hid her embarrassment under a lecture on table behaviour. Yet she had seen beneath the laughter a faint surmise.

Nothing daunted, Simon plunged on: 'Auntie Grace nearly got married once, but Douglas died. He fell off the rocks. I liked Douglas. He showed me some fox cubs once—'

Grace's fork fell with a tiny crash. The old chill despair washed over her. For some moments she could not raise her eyes.

Martin catechized Simon on knots already learned, successfully diverting the child's mind. A few minutes later he pushed back his chair. 'I've got something to show you in my microscope, Simon. Coming?'

'You bet!' Before Grace had lifted her eyes they left the room.

This was how it would be, she warned herself. She might hear Douglas's name any time without warning. She must brace herself to bear it, that was all.

As for Martin, he might be an 'overgrown schoolboy' in Alec's sober eyes, but his quick intuitive sympathy had warmed her heart.

She finished her coffee, saw Simon off to the village school, then crossed the hall to the surgery. Martin was right about the muddle. The records were out of order, the desk overflowing and the samples cupboard a shambles. She found an overall and set to work.

Alec's practice was a large and scattered one, including the in-bye and out-bye farms of the hills. He held a daily morning surgery and an evening one thrice weekly. Once a month he held a maternity and child welfare clinic in the church hall. Dedicated to his patients, with a deep understanding of their special problems, he had no ambition beyond serving them to the limit of his strength. Already Grace had guessed that Martin was unlikely to see such serious involvement. His nature, though good-humoured and kindly, was a lighter one.

The doctors followed a duty rota for surgery. This morning it was Alec's turn, while Martin made a round of calls. Some eight or nine patients gathered in the waiting-room, a small annexe built on to the north side of the house. Burly shepherds, buxom mothers and patient-eyed farm wives alike greeted her by name, voiced their pleasure at her return. She was touched and cheered by their welcome.

She worked at the little hatch between waiting-room and dispensary, calling out names, finding records, handling prescriptions. Only one face was unfamiliar to her, that of a well-set-up, grey-haired man with an educated accent.

He was the last to go. Alec yawned and stretched himself, then got up from his desk. 'I've some urgent letters I'd like you to type next, Gay. I've got sadly into arrears since Isobel had to go.' Grace sensed something odd in the hesitation that followed.

'I suppose you noticed our last patient was MacEwan from Peppercorn?'

'From . . . I took his name, but I didn't realize—'

'He has had a septic thumb, but this will be his last visit – in more senses than one.' Alec met her gaze uneasily.

'Alec, what's wrong?' A thread of panic wormed through her.

'It seems they're leaving Peppercorn, Gay. Their lease has expired and his wife doesn't want to renew. She finds it too isolated.'

'You mean—'

'He told the agent their decision some time ago, and he got in touch with the owner. . . . I'm sorry, Grace. It seems Ellis Ridley is coming back to live there, permanently, this time. He's expected in about a fortnight.'

CHAPTER TWO

Grace held on to the desk for support.

'Ellis Ridley – coming back?' Dismay swept in a full tide.

'Grace, I'm sorry. I know how you must feel. I only wish I'd known earlier.' Alec added on a crisper note: 'All the same, taking the long view, it might not be such a bad thing.'

'Not such . . . Alec, are you out of your mind?'

'No, I'm not. I'm sorry, but this has to be said. It's a year and a half ago now, and though this may sound brutal, Abbotshaws has mostly forgotten the scandal around Douglas's death.'

'They may forget, but I never shall, Alec. And if what you say is true, he doesn't deserve to escape so lightly. It's all wrong that a man who behaved like that should be accepted again by his neighbours.'

Alec said quietly: 'You forget you loved Douglas – they didn't.' He began to fill his pipe. 'Understand this – I do sympathize with the way you feel. I can't say I'd fly any flags for the man myself, but as far as ostracizing him goes – I'm sorry, but you're on your own.'

'You mean you'd associate with him? Meet him at your friends' houses?'

'I wouldn't go out of my way to do so, but yes – if I couldn't ignore him without offending my friends, I would associate with him.'

She faced him in tearful, angry despair. 'You've changed, Alec. We always used to think the same, feel the same. . . .' Her voice broke.

He came to put an arm about her. 'I hate having to hurt you, Gay.' The use of the pet name was a measure of his feeling. 'But you can't expect to inject us all with your private venom for Ellis Ridley. As it is, there's no need to be so upset. You may never have to meet him. Or, knowing his unpredictable nature, he may grow restless after a month and disappear again. Just put him out of your mind altogether.'

He gave her a final pat and left the surgery.

Grace began to tidy the desk, her hands moving blindly. 'Put him out of your mind altogether—'

How simple it sounded, and how grateful she would be to be able to do it. The crowning irony was that though Douglas's face was now fading from her memory, she could recall Ellis's without conscious effort; those enigmatic eyes, his monumental self-possession, the dark flawed features so like Douglas and yet so unlike. Try as she might, she could not rid her mind of him. He came to haunt her dreams, adding to the score she already held against him of bitterness and despairing anger.

Alec could blandly assert that she might never have to meet him, but her life with Douglas had led her into new social connections which had often included Ellis. She could think of two families at least from whose hospitality it would be difficult to escape, and they too were friends of Ellis.

If, as Alec said, the people of the district had conveniently forgotten the circumstances of Douglas's death, it was just as likely they might underestimate her feelings.

These thoughts harried her as she worked. When she had typed the letters for Alec she spent another hour in bringing order to the surgery and dispensing-room. The cries of the children released from the village school reminded her that Simon would be in to lunch. For his sake she must appear cheerful.

He trudged in at the gate, his socks at half-mast, his face smudged with coloured chalk under the bright tousled hair. Watching from the living-room window Grace saw his woebegone glance, missing his mother's face. Then he spied Grace and grinned. She met him in the hall with a hug.

'Well, what have you been up to this morning?' she demanded.

'I did chalking.'

'Yes, I can see that,' she teased.

'And old Purvis – that's the headmaster – made the big boys stop teasing us. We had a circus and we were the horses and they hit us with sticks.'

'Did they?' Grace was concerned.

He beamed. 'Yes – it was great!'

She laughed. 'Run and wash your hands, then you can see to your menagerie while I help dish up lunch.'

'Will you come to see Nelson and Napoleon after?'

'Only if you leave a clean plate.'

He rushed off. Jess came through the hall, a table-cloth in her hand. 'My, it's doing him good, having you here, Miss Haydon.'

'I hope so. But I feel a poor substitute for his mother. Here, Jess, let me do that. I know where everything is.'

Jess relinquished the cloth, a shade reluctantly. Grace laid the table, feeling calmer now. Maybe she needed this reminder that Simon deserved a stable mother-substitute.

She went to help Jess dish up, but was kept firmly in her place. 'I'm no' quite ready yet. You'd best take a seat for five minutes.'

From the window Grace saw an estate car pull into the old stable yard. Jess peered over her shoulder. 'There's Doctor Finch. He's punctual, for once.' She turned from the cooker, a ladle in her hand. Her solid weatherbeaten face held a hint of doubt.

'You'll have heard Mr. Ridley's coming back?'

'Yes.' Grace strove to keep her voice casual.

'Aye, I can see it's upset you. Well, it was bound to.'

'It won't upset me as long as I don't have to meet him, Jess.' Grace could see Martin Finch whistling as he gave a polish to his car. He looked relaxed and carefree. She was like that once, she remembered with a pang.

'You still hold that business against him, then?' Jess's voice had stiffened.

'Wouldn't you?' Grace flared. 'You were fond of Douglas, Jess. You know you were.'

'Aye. He was a canny lad, Douglas. But Mr. Ridley was my employer, when all's said and done. I'm right sorry I won't be able to work for him again.'

Jess's tone held more than a hint of anxiety for Ellis Ridley's welfare. It touched Grace on the raw.

'You mean you would actually have worked for him again, after what he did?'

'And what did he do, Miss Haydon? Beyond not answering the door?'

Grace felt her cheeks flame. 'That wasn't all, was it?'

'So folks say. And I'm no' doubting it. He likes women, does Mr. Ridley. Aye, and they like him.' Jess stirred the soup vigorously. 'I wouldn't say I approved of all he did. But I've no call to complain of his treatment of me. He was a good master, kind and considerate. And what's done is done. Hard talk'll no' bring back Mr. Douglas.'

She bustled to the sink to strain the potatoes, her brawny arms braced against the weight of the heavy pot. 'It's been a muckle grief to you, Miss Haydon. I'm no' gainsaying that. But to hold his death against Mr. Ridley – why, what good does that do? Best forgive and forget.'

'It's easy to talk, Jess,' Grace said stiffly. As she helped carry in the dishes she reminded herself that Jess was the second person that morning to make light of Ellis Ridley's faults. Was there no one but herself to condemn him? How could people be so lax, so forgetful?

She sat down to lunch with Simon and the two men, bracing herself to appear normal. Alec held a solemn discussion with his son on the merits of Miss Ogle, his teacher. Martin turned with a smile to Grace. 'Busy morning?'

She nodded, smiling. 'And you?'

'You can say that again. I've cases of mumps and chickenpox blooming like the flowers of spring.'

'It's the time of year for it,' she agreed.

'Then I've got a rare case of lamb fever.'

'Lamb fever? What on earth—'

He laughed. 'Jess's old father. You must go to see him, Grace. He's just like a picture by Landseer, sitting up in bed with his dog beside him on an old plaid shawl. Yes, he has lamb fever. It's just the time of year he used to be up in the lambing folds. Poor old boy – he'd tell me yarns by the hour if I'd the time to listen.'

Simon looked up, his spoon arrested in his soup. 'Did he tell you about the goats?'

'Keeps goats, does he?'

'No!' The child's voice was scathing. 'I mean *wild* goats. There used to be a herd of them up in the hills – he told me. Gosh, I wish I'd seen them. That's why they call it Goatshiels—'

Alec glanced at Grace. 'All right, old man. What about finishing this soup?'

'Wild goats?' Martin echoed. 'You mean – recently?' Bewildered, he turned to Alec.

'Oh yes, comparatively recently. I've spoken to one or two in-bye farmers who knew of several small herds up to the end of the last war, and as near here as Thrunton crags. I've heard there is still a remnant of one of the herds up by Yeavering Bell, but never actually met anyone who has seen them.' He glanced at his son and added firmly, 'For all practical purposes they could be said to be extinct now.'

'Old Will knows all about them,' Simon put in eagerly. 'He's actually seen them!'

Alec spoke dryly to Martin: 'And why the smile?'

'Sorry!' Martin grinned. 'Just a thought. I was told you all wore skins up here. Maybe I wasn't so far out – wild beasts now!'

'You ought to be here during the snows. Then you'd really know you're in a primitive land, my lad . . . By the way, did you call on old Mrs. Beattie at Heatherhouses?'

'No, actually I didn't. I knew it wasn't urgent, and I shall be that way tomorrow.'

Alec eyed him coolly. 'I'd prefer you to follow my directions as far as possible. It's a boggy road to Heatherhouses, little more than a track. Given two days' rain, which is certainly on the way, and it'll be almost impassable.'

Martin looked abashed. When Jess had been in with the sweet Alec went on: 'Doctoring up here isn't quite the same as attending the dear old ladies of Kensington. We have to be not only medical men but weather experts, highway inspectors and sometimes clairvoyants. Otherwise we'd never be able to decide which farmer with a coronary will kill himself with overwork, or which expectant mother will have to be confined at home because the land rover's bogged and the telephone line's down. So never take anything for granted.'

'Sorry, Doctor Haydon.' But Martin looked a little downcast. When Alec refused coffee and left with Simon for a walk round the garden, Grace said softly:

'You mustn't mind Alec. He's just terribly conscientious – always was. And he's worried about Isobel. ... He's really quite pleased with you. He told me so.'

Martin glowed. 'Well, that's a load off my mind. I was beginning to wonder how many more bloomers I'd make.'

'He was always a perfectionist, even as a boy. When he taught me to ride our family pony he was so particular about my hands and seat that some days we got no further than the stable yard ... until I lost my temper and told him I wasn't training for the Derby.'

'And does that happen often – you losing your temper?'

She smiled and shook her head. 'If I do, I always feel such a fool afterwards. You're pretty easy-going yourself, aren't you?'

'In my case it's laziness. Flying off the handle never seems worth the effort.' He went on: 'Anyway, thanks for telling me your brother is reasonably satisfied.' He grinned. 'That gives me confidence to go on – and make more mistakes.'

She laughed, then broke off confusedly under his bright glance. 'You should laugh more often, Grace. Sometimes you look as if you had all the cares of the world on your shoulders.'

'There are – reasons.' She was painfully embarrassed.

'Yes, I know.' He became very busy folding his table-napkin. 'I heard about it. It was shocking bad luck.'

The casual phrase, so lightly said, might have hurt her, but she was sensitive enough to realize it covered a genuine sympathy. Next moment the conversation was broken by Simon, who came to demand her presence at the guinea-pig hutches.

During the next few days Grace found many difficulties in her new routine. She was anxious to shoulder as many of Alec's burdens as possible, to be a mother-substitute for Simon and to keep a smoothly-running household. After more than a year of undemanding work and abundant leisure she found the days brimful and heavily demanding. It was easy to see how Isobel had cracked under the strain when already weakened by illness.

The biggest thorn in her side was Jess Robson. Used as Jess had been to complete charge of Peppercorn, she was inclined to rule at Lintlaw House, and fretted Grace with constant advice.

'If I were you, I wouldn't give the men too many cold suppers, Miss Haydon. A man needs a hot meal after his day's work. And if you haven't the time I could quite easily do a dish or two ready for you to heat up – a good stew with dumplings, or a casserole of chicken.'

Grace's protest that Alec preferred cold suppers made little impression. There came further advice on the sorting of the laundry, the arrangement for changing bed-linen, even the management of the larder.

'Deed now, if you haven't moved those plates again! I like everything just as I've always had it, Miss Haydon. Then, when I've the lunch to cook, I've just to put my hand out and find what I want.'

Grace could dig her heels in when necessary. 'Yes, but I have meals to get too, and I find this arrangement suits me.'

Then would come the inevitable: 'All right, Miss Haydon. Suit yourself, of course.' Much clashing of pans and cutlery would follow. 'But at Pepppercorn, now—'

At last Grace flared: 'But you're not at Peppercorn now, Jess. And I don't particularly want my brother's household modelled on Ellis Ridley's.'

The words were out before she could stop them. Jess raised her sandy eyebrows. 'My, you *are* in a taking! ... I mind the time when you used to say how well I ran Peppercorn.'

This prickle of contention between them regarding Peppercorn was, Grace realized, only the surface ruffle of a much deeper turmoil. She resented Jess's loyalty to Ellis Ridley, Jess in her turn would brook no criticism of him. But neither woman wanted disharmony. Both had too much concern for the happiness of the household. Grace learned to bite her tongue, to steer the conversation away from dangerous channels; and sometimes Jess looked volumes but kept her own counsel.

Soon Alec began to notice that Grace had little leisure. One evening nearly a fortnight after her arrival he noticed her push her supper-plate aside. He spoke calmly:

'Don't hide your plate behind the daffodils, Grace. I can see you're not eating well. And you look tired. The truth is you're trying to do too much.'

She smiled. 'Oh, really, Alec – I only do what has to be done.'

'So did Isobel, and she's in hospital,' he retorted. 'Perhaps I needed her collapse to open my eyes. Now, Grace, do be sensible. Of course it's pleasant to have the house and surgery run on oiled wheels, to have Simon happy and cared for, but the strain is beginning to show. Tell me now, just how often have you been out of doors in the past week?'

She hesitated. 'I usually meet Simon out of school, and I play with him in the garden most evenings before surgery. Then I'm out in the village most days, shopping—'

'Exactly. In other words you've still been on the job. It won't do, you know. You must have some relaxation. There's no reason why you shouldn't get out during the afternoons before Simon comes home. Either Martin or I will be off duty if anyone telephones.'

Grace was silent, touched by his concern but a little mutinous. Men just did not realize the hundred and one domestic details which could pile up. She wished too that Alec had not lectured her before Martin.

'I'll try,' she said.

'You could always come out on the afternoon round, with either Martin or myself. It would give you a chance to meet up with old friends.'

Martin said impulsively: 'I'm going up Lorbottle way tomorrow. Why not come with me, Grace?'

'There you are!' Alec turned back to his supper, well satisfied. 'You'll be able to give him a lesson on country lore as you go along.'

'But if I'm late back for Simon—'

Alec frowned. 'I shall be here. Simon won't expire for a little lack of attention. I have no intention of allowing you to be a slave to him.'

Martin gave her a sympathetic smile. She found herself returning it. Good old Alec, he meant well, even if he was a bit heavy-handed sometimes. And it would be good to get away from it all, even for an hour or two.

Next day was bright and blustering, with high white clouds and intermittent sunshine. The wind was still wintry, but the last grey streaks of snow had disappeared. As the car sped towards the Thrunton heights, where dark firs crowned the crags, Grace felt herself relax for the first time in days.

'Glad you came?' Martin asked.

'Oh yes. Alec's right, I suppose. It's only too easy to get bogged down in domestic affairs.' She wound down the window. 'Hear that? In London I used to dream of that sound – the cries of new-born lambs. . . . No, you're looking the wrong way – that lambing pen over there. It's a hard time for the shepherds – and their wives. They'll be nursing the weakling lambs in their kitchens.'

Martin groaned. 'Sheep are rapidly becoming my Waterloo. I'm getting scared to open my mouth. I always ask all the wrong questions. Half the time I don't know what my patients are talking about. What with tups and rams and wethers and gimmers and ewes. . . . Then just to confuse the issue they pronounce it "yowes".'

'You'll learn,' she teased. 'The northern shepherds have their own names – they're different again in the south. A southerner coming up here to the sheep sales has to have the catalogue translated.'

'I'm not surprised. . . . What's that big place over there?'

'Callaly Castle. It's a rebuilt Border fortress. There's rather a queer legend attached to it.'

'Go on. I'm all ears.'

'Well, it seems the lord and his lady had a dispute as to the site of the original castle. He wanted it on the heights and she wanted it down on the level. He began building, but she disguised one of her menials as a wild boar, and each night he pulled down the stones the lord's men had built during the day. There's an old verse about it. It goes:

"Callaly Castle, built on the height,
Up in the day and down in the night.
Builded down in the shepherd's shaw,
It will stand for aye and never fa'." '

Martin laughed. 'I see he took it to heart. It's down on the level. . . . "Up in the day and down in the night" – most of my castles in the air have the same fate.'

'Mine too.' The shadow returned to her face. Several miles later they drove under bleak ranges of foothills into the main valley of Coquetdale, where the river looped endlessly on its way to the sea. To the south-west loomed the flat-topped heights of the Simonside range, grape-blue under the dark cloud-shadows, and changing contour with every turn of the road.

Martin broke silence to say: 'You were very much in love with this Douglas Ridley, weren't you? Snub me if I'm talking out of turn.'

'I don't mind talking about it – to you.' She went

on: 'Everyone thinks I should be over it by now. Even Alec gets impatient with me. But it was such a senseless tragedy.'

'Doctor Haydon told me some of it and Angela filled in. Something to do with the half-brother, wasn't it?'

'Yes.'

'And he's expected back any day now? I can see it's tough on you.' He hesitated. 'Angela seems to think the scandal was a lot of fuss about nothing.'

'Angela didn't lose the man she loved!' Grace protested. 'It's always easy to make light of other people's tragedies.'

'Oh, I don't suppose she thought very deeply about it.' He spoke airily. 'Clumsy of me to mention it.'

He swung the car into a side track and a few moments later through the gateway of a farm steading. 'Percy Adams,' he recapped. 'Bad case of shingles. Want to come in? You know them, don't you?'

'Yes, I know them. But I won't come in. I'll take a walk down the lane.'

She experienced a cowardly panic at the thought of meeting the Adamses. They had known Douglas so well, and Jack, the eldest son, had ridden with him at the point-to-point. They would give her a kind welcome, but somehow she could not face them. Not yet.

She idled down the stony track, no sound about her but the piping of the wind, the plaintive cries of the sheep and the curlews. The wind lifted her hair, blew cold and fresh against her face. Despite reminders of Douglas a wash of happiness came. How often in London had she ached for the hills, for that same lone crying of the wind. Alec may have been right. In time the familiar scenes of home might have worked their own benediction; instead the shadow of Ellis Ridley loomed again. She was not to be allowed escape from her tragedy. He would stir again all the old half-buried emotions of that time.

Martin hailed her from the car. She retraced her steps. 'How is Mr. Adams?' she called.

'Picking up. The rash is fading, but there's some debility. That's to be expected.' He consulted his note-book. 'Now, where next? Oh yes, Whinney Edge and old Mrs. Morton.'

They followed a narrow side-road climbing steadily through lonely moorland. The rough track took several blind turns round the shoulders of the hills. This, to Grace, was the most significant road in the world. It led to Peppercorn, and she knew every inch of it as she knew her own heart.

Suddenly came the sound of another car approaching at speed. Martin tensed. Round the next bend came a large black saloon. With a smothered curse Martin wrenched the wheel over and slammed on his brakes. The car drew up with a shuddering jolt on the brink of the ditch.

'The man's crazy!' Martin got out, and somewhat shaken, Grace followed. The other car had slewed sideways and also stopped. A tall man and a blonde girl got out.

Grace felt the blood drain from her face. The girl was Angela Forster, the man, now approaching Martin with a cool air of command, was Ellis Ridley.

'You all right?' he called. 'Sorry I was taking all the road. It's not often we meet anyone coming this way—'

He broke off, seeing Grace. For a moment he seemed nonplussed, but held her gaze steadily: 'Well, hallo!'

Grace remained white and silent.

Martin exploded: 'I happen to be a doctor, on my

way to visit a patient. Seems I'm lucky not to be a patient myself!'

Through her racing, tumultuous thoughts Grace found herself surprised at the strength of his anger. Now she heard Angela speak:

'Hallo, Martin. ... For heaven's sake relax – no harm done, is there?' She nodded coolly to Grace, then turned to Ellis. 'This is Doctor Finch, Doctor Haydon's new partner.'

Ellis Ridley smiled. 'Sorry again, old man. And if you want to make anything of this, my name's Ridley.'

Martin glanced at Grace, seeing for the first time her dumb wretchedness. 'You've upset Miss Haydon!' He slid a supporting hand under her elbow.

Ellis Ridley was watching her. For an earth-shaking moment the angle of his features, a trick of the light, gave her an image, not of himself, but Douglas. Then he moved again, the scar became evident; she saw again the harsher profile, the sharper planes of Ellis.

His stance was easy and assured, his hands in the pockets of a casual jacket. The expression of his eyes was enigmatic.

'Was it as bad as that – the shock of the swerve, I mean? If so, I apologize again, Grace.'

Still she could find no words. 'Angela told me you were home,' he went on. 'I was sorry to hear about Mrs. Haydon.'

Martin broke in: 'I doubt if Grace feels equal to social chit-chat, Ridley. I think she would prefer to go back to the car. It might have occurred to you that it was shock of another kind.'

Ellis Ridley's dark brows lifted. His searching gaze moved to Grace again, then back to Martin. 'I begin to comprehend you. ... Come, Angela, we mustn't upset Miss Haydon.'

Angela flashed a smile at Martin, ignored Grace. As they turned away her voice wafted on the wind: 'It seems she still sees you as the black sheep, after a year in the bright lights. . . . And did you notice – her looks have quite gone—'

Martin helped Grace back to the car. They both sat in silence for a moment, hearing the others drive away.

'So much for your afternoon's outing!' he said at last. 'Damn Ridley and his condescension!'

Grace roused herself, surprised at his anger. 'Don't worry about me, Martin. . . . It *was* a shock, seeing him again, but I'll have to get used to it. And he was right about there never being anyone on this road. Douglas always used to belt along like a racing driver —'

'That's still no excuse—'

'Please, Martin, forget it!' Her plea was so heartfelt he said no more, but drove on towards Whinney Edge. Gradually she controlled the storm of feeling Ellis Ridley's presence had aroused, but the unrest went deep. How strange that it had taken only one glance at his face to recall, after vain months, the vivid memory of Douglas. This enemy could bring her the greatest gift she could seek, and yet in finding it she found too the greatest revulsion. One moment he was Douglas, bringing a memory of rapture, the next he was the nightmare behind the dream.

And stranger still – that first sight of Angela beside him had brought her the pangs of a wild false jealousy, as if Douglas had returned from the dead to flaunt unfaithfulness.

She was very little aware of the farms and lonely cottages they visited next. Martin was silent again on the drive home down the gradual heights of the moor towards Abbotshaws.

That evening she had her usual chat with Simon before he went to sleep. He sat up in bed drinking his cocoa, his freckled face angelically clean under the rusty mop of hair. First of all came an earnest discussion on hospital routine, the speculation as to what his mother was likely to be doing at that time.

'Having her supper, I expect. And she may be listening to the radio. But more probably she's thinking about you, and wondering if you brushed your teeth properly. Did you?'

He dipped his face in the mug. 'Fifty-five strokes, I counted. Mummy used to sit on my bed too, but she told me animal stories. I don't suppose you know any?'

'Just *Brer Rabbit* and *The Wind in the Willows*.'

'They're not bad, especially Toad. But I meant stories about real animals – true ones, like old Will tells.'

'You mean about wild goats?'

He nodded, his eyes bright. 'He told me about a badger's funeral he saw once. Did you know badgers bury their dead?'

'I believe I had heard that.'

'And once old Will saw a white fox – an albino. They're very rare, you know.'

'I'm sure they are.' She took his mug away. 'Have you ever seen the wild white cattle at Chillingham?'

He gave her a pitying glance. 'I saw them when I was *four*. But I'm more interested in wild goats. I asked Mr. Ridley about them today.'

Grace did a faint double-take. 'Mr. – Ridley?'

He settled back on his pillows, his hands behind his head. 'Yes, he's come back. Didn't you know? I was early out of school and he stopped his car to speak to me. I asked him to be sure to let me know if he ever sees any goats up there – at Goatshiels. They used to be there, you know. And they might come back. Old Will says—'

'I didn't know you'd seen Mr. Ridley,' Grace put in. 'Was Miss Forster with him?'

'Yes, but she didn't talk to me. She looked cross. I like Mr. Ridley, don't you? He promised to let me know if he ever sees any wild goats. And he gave me money for an ice-cream.'

Grace was startled. Seen through the child's eyes Ellis Ridley sounded almost human. Once again it seemed that everyone she knew was determined to admire the man.

'What else did he say?' she asked reluctantly.

'He asked me if I liked school, an' I told him about Nelson and Napoleon. He thought they were good names. He told me he had a guinea-pig once, called Samson, an' it had a wife called De – something.'

'Delilah?'

'Yes, I think that's right. Anyway, they escaped from the hutch and got out on the moor and went to live in an old rabbit warren. In the end there was a whole colony of them, gone wild.'

'I don't expect that worried Mr. Ridley,' Grace said sharply. 'He doesn't really care much about animals. You mustn't expect everyone to be as interested as you are.'

'But Mr. Ridley—'

'Time to go to sleep now,' she smiled, but her voice was firm. She felt she had heard enough about Ellis Ridley for one night.

It was a non-surgery night. Alec was away at Newcastle, visiting Isobel. He should just have arrived at the hospital by this time. Martin was out for an evening run in his car and probably a drink at some moorland pub. The house was peaceful and Grace settled down with a book in the living-room.

Ten minutes later she heard the surgery bell ring, and went to answer it. People often called for medicine on non-surgery nights, and there were several prescriptions waiting to be picked up.

She opened the opaque glass door of the waiting-room. Outside stood Ellis Ridley. She froze, unbelieving.

'Hallo again,' he said quietly. 'Sorry to trouble you, Grace, but I promised to pick up the tablets for Billy Middlemass. Are they ready?'

She said in some confusion: 'Will you come in? I'll just go and see.' In the small dispensary she found the tablets, stood a moment to compose herself, then went back. Ellis Ridley was standing before a poster exhorting mothers to have their children immunized.

'Here they are,' she said.

He took the package, surveyed her coolly. 'No after-effects from your fright this afternoon, I hope?' There was a faint tinge of sarcasm behind the words.

'None at all, thank you.'

'You're very distant, Grace. I didn't exactly expect to be welcomed with open arms, but must you be so hostile?'

'That's something you must ask yourself, Mr. Ridley.' She spoke unsteadily.

'*Mr*. Ridley now? You used to call me Ellis.'

'That was a long time ago.'

The room seemed peculiarly airless. He had closed the door and his personality seemed overwhelming in the narrow room. She could hear no sound but the restless cawing of rooks about the church tower. Time had halted and his scrutiny grown merciless.

'As you say – a long time ago,' he said at last. 'When I first saw you I thought of the fairies of Brinkburn. I envied Douglas. But you've changed, Grace. Or must it be Miss Haydon now?'

She jerked her eyes away from that mesmeric stare. 'It doesn't matter, because I shall do my best to avoid you. We have nothing to say to each other.'

'You are mistaken. I may in the future have quite a lot to say to you. And you won't find it so easy to avoid me, for I see no reason to co-operate.'

'No reason?' She was stung to anger. 'You never denied your negligence the night Douglas—'

'I never denied it, true. But I feel no guilt and I have no intention of wearing a permanent hair-shirt just to satisfy Grace Haydon.'

'You must have been born without a conscience!' She was at white heat now, and trembling.

He said harshly: 'Douglas is dead. And nothing you say or think can bring him back. *I* am very much alive and determined to take up the threads of my life where I left off – whether you like it or not! I hope that's clear?'

She was silent. It seemed for a moment that his eyes were shadowed by grief, then he shrugged. 'I'm due to dine at the Grange, so I'll say good-night. I imagine you want to get back to the company of Sir Galahad – in other words your callow young doctor.'

Her face flamed. 'Doctor Finch is a friend – nothing more. You're insulting!'

His smile was bleak. 'I'm sorry. Friend or not, there was a time when I might have envied him. But the radiant fairy has lost her radiance. Bitterness hasn't improved you, Grace. Take care it doesn't destroy you!'

His eyes blazed in challenge, but again his likeness to Douglas weakened her resistance. In the shadowed dusk the differences of profile and expression were almost undetectable. Her subconscious instincts brought their own reaction, the glory and rapture of the past engulfing her without mercy. She almost reached out her hands towards him.

Then he turned to go and was clearly Ellis again. The door clicked behind him and she was alone.

For days that scene stayed vividly in her mind. His accusation of bitterness both angered and dismayed her.

What else did he expect? she asked herself.

To smother that bitterness would seem like treachery to Douglas. And as to it destroying her, she hoped her sense of balance would save her from such a fate. She marvelled daily that he, who had so much blame at his door, should criticize *her*. It was typical of the man's arrogance.

Meanwhile the rain prophesied by Alec swept the vale for days on end. The crags were hidden in sodden mists, and the shepherds at the lambing pens had the added hazard of wet lying conditions for the in-lamb ewes. The surgery was busy with colds and bronchial complaints, and Simon restless and fractious at being kept indoors.

Grace found her nerves fraying, though she tried not to show it. She tried to spend more time with Simon, and found him happiest when she shared his reading of his natural history books, and entered on long solemn discussions on the habits of roe deer and the behaviour of seal pups.

Then overnight came a spell of windless warmth. The vale flushed with new green, lambs tottered on ungainly legs. Early violets flourished in the sheltered garden behind Lintlaw House, and Simon ran in from school exultant at hearing his first cuckoo of spring.

From the hospital came reassuring news of Isobel's gradual progress. Grace was anxious to visit her, but there were difficulties. If she went with Alec on non-surgery evenings, this would leave no one with Simon, as Martin would be on call. It was Jess who found a solution.

'There's my neighbour's lass, Peggy Everitt. She's a canny bairn, just sixteen. She works up at Forsters during the day, but she's no' a one for going out at nights. Simon knows her, so it wouldn't be like having a stranger in.'

Grace agreed and one evening the following week Peggy arrived as sitter-in. She was a fair well-built girl with timid blue eyes but a ready smile. Her adolescent gawkiness was still very evident, and Grace strove to put her at her ease.

'It was good of you to help us out, Peggy. I've left you a supper-tray and some magazines if you don't want TV. If Doctor Finch has to go out you might take down any telephone messages. You don't mind, do you?'

'No, Miss Haydon, I'll manage fine. It'll be a fair treat just to sit down. We're spring-cleaning up at the Grange, and I've been run off my feet the day.'

Grace turned to the mirror to pat her hair, which was soft and unruly after shampooing.

'You've right bonny hair, Miss Haydon,' Peggy

ventured. 'My sister's is that colour – she's away from home now, working in Manchester. She takes after Dad, but I'm fair like Mam.'

'We'd better swop, then. I've always had a yen to be a blonde!' Grace turned to add: 'Do you work full-time at the Grange, then?'

'Aye, I'm up there by eight in the morning, and finish about six, unless they've a dinner-party on. Then I'm there all hours.'

Grace remembered that Mrs. Forster, Angela's mother, had the reputation of being mean and a hard driver where domestics were concerned. She felt sorry for the girl.

Peggy chatted on: 'Miss Angela's right pleased with herself now Mr. Ridley's back. He's been up at the Grange quite a bit. My mam thinks there might be a wedding before long.'

Grace stiffened. She found herself unable to chat about Ellis Ridley, and turned to other topics. Later, driving with Alec over the moors towards the A.1. road to Newcastle, she wondered again about Peggy's artless snippet of gossip. Ellis and Angela would be well matched, she decided; his hard arrogance plus her cool disdain. Each would get the partner they deserved.

It was when she began to imagine Angela as mistress of Peppercorn that her thoughts were severely jolted. This was an unexpected pain. Although she had been fairly near to Peppercorn on several occasions when driving with Martin, she had flinched from seeing the actual house. Once it had meant everything to her as her future home. Now Ellis Ridley reigned there alone.

Yet the lonely house on the heights still drew her with a powerful magic, both waking and sleeping.

Only the night before she had dreamed she was walking again with Douglas in its walled garden. Then it became a game of hide and seek among the High Stones, Douglas climbing away from her, laughing and beckoning her on. The dream shivered into nightmare as he lost his footing, pitched headlong to the ravine below. . . .

Peppercorn had given her both happiness and tragedy. Its memory was twined irrevocably round her heart, and some part of her refused to be reconciled to seeing Angela as its mistress.

At the hospital she waited until Alec had spent half an hour alone with Isobel, then she presented herself at the ward. Alec excused himself for a chat with the house physician and the two girls were left alone.

'You're sitting up now! This *is* a step forward!' Grace bent to kiss her sister-in-law. 'I've brought you some violets from Lintlaw. I knew you'd prefer them to hothouse flowers.'

Isobel buried her face in the fragrant posy. She looked less wasted now and had a hint of colour. With her dark hair on her shoulders and a rosy bed-jacket she looked almost a beauty, though her charm had always lain in personality rather than good features.

'They're lovely! Don't tell me where you picked them – let me guess. On the bank by the summer-house?'

'Right first time. And Simon helped me pick them.'

'How *is* he, Grace? I know Alec always says he's fine, but he could be making light of things. Is he really quite happy?'

Grace smiled. 'He is – and I should know. Of course he misses you, but he *has* adjusted to having me around instead. And school is a big help.'

Patiently she answered the young mother's anxious questions, and at last Isobel relaxed again on her pillows. 'Sorry to put you through the third degree, Grace. I know we're terribly lucky to have you. But I always imagine he misses me as much as I miss him.' Her voice grew unsteady. 'You know I can bear being ill. I can stand the monotony and the injections and the drugs, but no one warned me what would be the worst part – being homesick for Lintlaw and Abbotshaws. I know just how wonderful it must be now, with lambs everywhere and the birds nesting. And soon the swallows will be back. You know they always nest in the old stable. Simon waits for them every year.'

'I know,' Grace smiled. 'Perhaps you'll be home sooner than you think. I hear from Alec you're making really good progress?'

'Oh yes. Mr. Sutcliff – he's the chest consultant – was very pleased with my last batch of X-rays. There was some trouble at first over the strep. injections – a skin reaction. But that's cleared up now. In about a fortnight or so I may be allowed out of bed once a day – and believe me, that's progress!' She smiled ruefully. 'I sound like a perfect hypochondriac. . . . Let's forget about TB now, shall we? Did you know Simon wrote me a note?' She fingered a grubby piece of paper. 'Alec brought it. He told me Peggy Everitt was sitting-in. She's a bit slow but very dependable. You know she works at Forsters?'

Grace nodded.

'Have you seen much of Angela since you came?'

'No, not much.'

'I don't blame you. I don't know a single woman who likes her. She's a man's girl every time. Of course with her looks—'

Isobel broke off, then went on: 'I really thought she fancied Martin at first – that was before she knew Ellis was coming back. Now it's obvious she means to queen it at Peppercorn. Does Martin mind, do you know?'

Grace smiled a little. Isobel saw and said teasingly: 'Oh, I get it. He has other interests now. Do you like Martin?'

'Yes, I do – very much.'

'I'm glad. Especially now Ellis Ridley's back. It can't be easy for you, seeing him about. . . . Grace, I'm sorry! Does it really upset you to talk about him? Alec hinted as much. I'm sorry if I was clumsy.'

Grace patted her hand. 'Don't worry – it's something I've got to get used to, that's all.' She glanced at her watch. 'It's nearly time to go. Any more instructions for me – about Simon, I mean?'

'Just one. Do keep an eye on him, Grace. He's rather a wanderer. It's not that he's really disobedient, but when he gets an idea in his head he follows it to kingdom come. He has disappeared a few times already. Once he got on a bus, but the conductor put him off at Bridge of Aln, and he got a lift back with one of our patients. Then he went exploring up Callaly Crags, looking for eagles, of all things. He's too imaginative, that's the trouble. The line between dreams and reality – to Simon it's just a gossamer thread.'

'I know, and I'll do my best to act policeman. So far I've had no trouble.'

'I suppose I'm exaggerating, but a mother has a built-in sixth sense where danger is concerned. And believe me, it works overtime lying here.'

Alec came back, goodbyes were said, and Grace

effaced herself to allow husband and wife a last privacy.

In the car going home Alec was in good spirits. 'We should have engineered your visit earlier. Isobel seems much happier now she's had a talk with you and knows everything is going well. And I must say I feel more relieved myself.' He added gruffly: 'Whatever it cost you to come to us, Grace, we'll never forget it.'

'You'll have me in tears in a minute,' she laughed, but added quietly: 'I know you'd both do as much for me, any day.'

Alec began whistling to himself as the car left the busy Haymarket and mingled with the north-bound traffic. Grace realized it was a sound she had missed during recent weeks, and knew a warm satisfaction at its return. It seemed her efforts to help him were bearing fruit at last.

The following evening at surgery time Grace found an almost empty waiting-room. An old shepherd, a village mother with her baby, and a couple of youths comprised the patients. She lifted the hatch from the dispensary and took names. Old Jock Davidson had called for his wife's medicine.

'How is Mrs. Davidson now?' Grace asked.

'She's on the mend! And more than thankful, forbye!' He winked at her. 'These women, they're aye thinking it's the end o' the world if they have a stomach-ache.'

'And what about the old men?' the young mother demanded.

'Well now, we're made o' sterner stuff!' He pocketed the bottle, gave Grace a cheery nod and left.

The young wife, Mrs. Bishop, had brought her infant son for his diptheria immunization. Grace arranged further appointments and explained about the booster injections he would need later.

'It doesn't seem right, sticking needles in the bairn. But yon district nurse got on to me about it.'

'She was right, you know,' Grace smiled. 'Diphtheria would hurt baby far worse than a dozen needles.'

The first of the youths went into the surgery. He was followed later by Mrs. Bishop. The outer door opened to admit a further patient. Grace glanced up to see Angela Forster at the window, looking coolly beautiful in an expensive green sweater.

She held her left wrist supported in her right hand. After a brief amused glance at Grace's businesslike overall she said: 'I want to see Doctor Haydon. I think I've dislocated my wrist. Misty, my new mare, threw me this afternoon in the paddock, and Ellis positively ordered me to come along.'

Angela's striking green eyes held more than a hint of malice. Grace said quietly: 'You're next but one, then.'

Angela glanced at the waiting youth, and Grace remembered that he was stable-boy at the Grange.

'Oh, Bob won't mind if I go in first, will you, Bob?'

'No, Miss Forster, you can gan in ahead o' me.' But Grace saw the youth glance at his wrist-watch. She remembered the Alnwick bus was due in ten minutes. If Angela took his turn the lad might be deprived of his evening out.

Mrs. Bishop emerged from the surgery. Alec looked in. 'Next, please!' he called. As he retreated again Grace said firmly:

'You must take your proper turn, Bob. The doctor

will have your file ready.'

He flashed her a grateful look, then his face reddened under Angela's affronted stare. When he had gone Angela walked up to the window again.

'Quite the little dictator, aren't you? I suppose you wouldn't be delaying me because you know Ellis is waiting?'

Grace stared, her heart skipping a beat. 'I don't know what you mean.'

'Oh, I think you do.' Angela's smile was barbed. 'I saw the way you looked at him when we met on the moor road. He's terribly like Douglas at times, isn't he? . . . And wasn't it odd that you should come back just before Ellis did? I suppose you got wind of his coming?'

Grace felt the blood drain from her face. 'You must be out of your mind,' she stammered. 'Ellis Ridley is the very last man I'd be likely to want! The only reason I agreed to come back was because I was so sure he was still away.'

Angela hesitated, her eyes suspicious. 'That's your story, is it? But you did your best to waylay him in here the other night.'

'Is that what he told you?'

'Not quite. But I can read between the lines. . . . And I know *you*, darling. You even hung on to Douglas like a leech, though everyone knew about—'

Grace broke in, her anger spilling over: 'Please don't talk to me about Douglas. And try to get it into your head that I can't bear Ellis Ridley's company!'

Angela shrugged, icily composed again. 'Really, what a flap about nothing! Can't you take a joke?'

'I don't think you *were* joking.'

'Oh, you know me! I can't resist needling people.

You always were so intense, Grace. Forget it.' Angela turned away to go into the surgery as the stable-lad came out.

Alone again, Grace struggled with her whirling thoughts. *Had* Angela been joking? If so, it was the kind of sadistic teasing she had always enjoyed. Years ago she had always chosen the most timid village children for her calculated baiting. Grace knew this well, for she had been one of them.

Joking or not, she wondered exactly what Angela had meant to say about Douglas. . . . 'You hung on like a leech, though everyone knew. . . .'

Knew what? What had Angela meant to say? She felt oddly disturbed.

All at once she was painfully conscious of Ellis Ridley waiting outside. What had he told Angela about her? It seemed that, whether she liked it or not, she was destined to become involved with him.

CHAPTER THREE

Two days later Grace was shopping in the village when Simon joined her from school.

'Hallo, Auntie Grace! Isn't it hot?' He flapped his windcheater in an exaggerated gesture.

It was in fact a cold spring day of dark rushing cloud and intermittent showers, but Grace rightly interpreted the remark.

'You must need an ice-cream, then?'

'A raspberry lolly, actually.'

They visited the post-office, where ices could be bought along with stamps. Simon had his lolly and persuaded Grace to join him.

'You *bite* yours!' he accused her, as they walked homewards. 'You should lick round it with your tongue, like I do. It lasts longer.'

Grace declined the experiment. Raspberry lollies were rather daunting refreshment anyway, but she attacked hers manfully, sensing that as far as Simon was concerned, a lolly eaten alone had small emotional value.

They reached the old stone cottage, one-storied, where Jess lived. Behind the low garden wall was a brave show of early wallflowers and narcissi. A huge bush of feathery Lads' Love guarded the door.

Jess waved from the window, then came to the door. 'Will you no' come in a minute, Miss Haydon?'

They turned in at the gate. Jess whispered from the doorstep: 'My father does enjoy having the bairn in. And he'd like to see you again, I know.'

The high beamed living-room was warm and pleasant, the stone-flagged floor almost covered with pegged rugs. A double bed occupied the corner to left of the fireplace and here lay old Will, propped up by pillows, his wooden mat-frame on the bed before him. On a plaid rug at the foot of the bed lay the old collie, head between paws. He raised it to gaze at the visitors, his eyes bright but calm, then subsided again in sleep.

'Now, Father, here's Miss Haydon and the bairn come to see you.'

The old man carefully removed his spectacles and smiled at them. His rugged face was still alert, his eyes benign.

'It's grand to see ye again, Miss Haydon. I was hale and hearty last time we met, but with this arthritis in my hip I'm like a sick auld ram.'

Grace shook hands. 'I'm sorry you're laid up, but I see you keep busy.' She admired the half-finished mat in the frame.

Simon pored over it. 'Haven't you done a lot, Mr. Robson?' He spelled out the coloured text. "The Lord is my—" Is it "Shepherd" next?'

Old Will nodded. 'Aye, it's my favourite text, laddie. Now, which colour would you put next? The red or the purple?'

Simon fingered the long strips of woollen material waiting to be pegged. He frowned in serious concentration. 'You've got red here, and there's green in between, so you could have purple next.'

'Purple it is, then.'

Grace turned to Jess, who was setting the kettle back on the trivet. 'This is the first time I've been in your cottage. I think it's lovely.' Her gaze went from the polished shepherd's crook over the mantelpiece to the china dogs on the shelf. The net curtains were a shimmer of white flanking a row of plants. On the far wall a hanging clock ticked peacefully.

'You'll take a cup of tea, Miss Haydon?' Jess threw a snowy cloth over the red plush one on the centre table. 'Aye, it's old-fashioned. But it's my father's place, when all's said and done, and I'd be a poor daughter if I changed anything Mother had set store by when she was here. ... Oh, you're looking at that photo. I brought it with me when I left Peppercorn.'

Grace stood shocked at the sight of Douglas's laughing face, there on the wall. Jess unhooked the framed photograph and brought it over to the window.

'You can see it better here, Miss Haydon. But maybe you've a copy of your own?'

'Not this one.' Grace spoke faintly. In the background, but seeming far away, she heard the voices of old Will and Simon, discussing Moss, the collie. She heard the hissing of the kettle, the sound of a tractor in the village street; but in imagination she was far back in time, taken there by a camera's magic which had captured for ever Douglas's bold, winning smile. He stood holding the bridle of his favourite mare, Black Bess, his hair and the mare's mane windblown alike.

Jess breathed heavily over her shoulder. 'That was the day he won at the point-to-point, Miss Haydon – the year he died, it was. Mr. Ridley took the photo. I well remember he said after the funeral – this is the way I prefer to remember him.'

'What did he mean, Jess?' Grace's eyes were still fixed on the photograph.

Jess spoke with some reserve. 'Well, as you know, they didn't always see eye to eye. Nor did Mr. Ridley always hold with his brother's ways.'

She turned to the table to set out violet-speckled cups and a pat of new butter.

Grace said in some heat: 'The feeling was mutual, surely? And I think Ellis had less reason than Douglas to disapprove.'

Jess took the photograph back. 'There might have been faults on both sides, as you say.' But her words lacked conviction.

Grace felt the prick of tears. Faults? Douglas with faults? At this distance of time she would not concede even one. Again Jess's loyalty to the elder brother jarred.

'What happened to Black Bess?' she asked at last.

'Mr. Ridley sold him to a gentleman, Morpeth way. He needed the stable room.' Jess paused on her way to the back kitchen, raising her voice above Simon's prattle. 'I've heard he's thinking of setting up his own breeding stud, for hunters. He's on the lookout for a suitable farm hereabouts. So it looks like he means settling this time.'

Grace was startled. Ellis Ridley settling down? It looked as though the marriage rumour might be true.

Her thoughts went to Black Bess, the quiet winsome mare who had shared so many of her happy days. So Ellis Ridley had sold her, banished her from her home without a qualm. No doubt he had made a nice profit out of her. The thought stung.

She remembered the story of how he got his scar. It was more than ever obvious now that he had no thought for animals except as a business proposition. Perhaps Black Bess was lucky to escape such a master.

She stifled her pain and turned her attention to Simon, who was at his most wheedling.

'Tell me about the wild goats again, Mr. Robson – *please*!'

'You mustn't be a nuisance,' she warned him.

'Let the laddie alone, Miss Haydon. He's got an inquiring mind, d'ye see, and that's a thing to encourage.' His kindly smile took the sting from the rebuke. He turned to Simon.

'Aye, well, Simon, I was a young man then, with the strength o' ten. I was shepherd on the flanks o' the Cheviots, up beyond Wooler. I'd seen the wild goats many a time, up on the skyline, but never near enough for ma' liking. But this day I saw a sight I never forgot, forbye it was years ago, before the first world war.'

'You got near to one, didn't you?' Simon bounced on the bed-edge in his excitement.

'Aye, I did. I'd been after a strayed lamb in the clefts o' the rock. There was a wee hole nearby and I thought I spied something move. I could see it wasna' the lamb, and I was curious forbye. And when I looked close, here was this newborn wild kid.'

Simon's eyes shone. 'What was it like, Mr. Roberts?'

'I mind it as well if it was yesterday, ma laddie. He was darkish, between black and grey but with a white belly. He had black hairy pads on his forelegs. . . . Aye, and his ears were black too, long and drooping.'

Old Will knew the value of a dramatic pause. He nodded a few times, then went on:

'I guessed what had happened, d'ye see. He'd be into his second day. The first day a nanny goat'll no' leave her kid. She grazes just where she is until she gets the wee one on his feet, so she can move him if there's danger about. Then she'd urge him to the rocks by nightfall and find him a wee hole to sleep in. He'd sleep fast, well into the morning, so she'd take the chance to graze further out, to find all the food she could. That's how I knew she'd be about, watching me. And she could well be fierce if I touched her kid, so I got back up the hill, at the back of the wind, and hid mysel' in the bracken—'

'She came back, didn't she?'

'Aye, sure enough she did. She was a fine-looking beast hersel', with big yellow eyes and long chin whiskers. The kid was still sleeping, but she nosed him out and licked him all over. Then she gave him suck and started playing with him. Aye, that was a fine sight! . . . She was teaching him to stand on his hind legs and fight the air with his head. Ah, but then she got sound o' me!'

'Did you make a noise?' Simon was entranced.

'Aye, I did. Loosened a stone with ma foot. She listened a wee while, standing stock still, with her tail lying along her back. Then she snorted and rapped at the rock with her forefoot. She nosed the kid to his feet and they were away! He ran alongside her, on his spindly wee legs, and I watched them till they were out o' sight.'

He sighed, then smiled. 'That was the nearest I ever got to the wild goats. . . . My, but they were bonny, those two!' He turned to Grace with an old man's courtesy: 'Ye'll forgive my ramblings, Miss Haydon. But memories like this are all I have now.' He reached out to stroke his old collie. Moss licked his hand and slept again.

Simon roused himself from a kind of semi-trance. 'Gosh, you *are* lucky, Mr. Roberts. I wish I could see a wild goat's kid. Daddy says if I'd lived before the war I might have seen some at Thrunton Crags. That's as near as anything. Will they ever come back there, Mr.

Robson?'

'There's no telling, ma laddie. Wild creatures, now, they turn up sometimes where they're least expected – that's a fact.'

'Now, Father, you're no' to be filling the laddie's head with ideas,' Jess scolded. 'Sit in, Miss Haydon – and Simon over here. I'd like to know what you think of my bramble jelly. I fancy I got it a bit on the sweet side, last year.'

Grace too had been lost in a dream of the hills. How often, up at Peppercorn, had she and Douglas listened by the hour to the tales of local shepherds. Her longing for that lonely outpost of Coquetdale returned with frightening force. She was glad to drink her tea and talk with Jess of village affairs. The old man liked to take his meals in silence, and she did not notice that Simon too, intent on bread and jelly, was quieter than usual.

The following day, soon after four o'clock, Grace took a long involved telephone call from Top Riggs, an isolated farm. Having verified the list of symptoms and promised a call from Alec on his morning round, she took her scribbled notes to the surgery and copied them out more clearly in the call-book. The chime of the old clock on the wall told the half hour. She glanced up sharply. School had been out since four and she had not heard Simon come in.

Not that she felt any alarm. He was a confirmed dawdler and could be counted on to look for birds' nests, watch tractors at work, or even stop to play on the village green. Even so, he was usually hungry for his tea.

She left the house and looked down the village street.

No Simon in sight. She tried the stable-yard and the guinea-pig hutches. Still no Simon.

Martin appeared from the garage. 'Hallo – lost something?'

'Have you seen Simon anywhere?'

'No. Isn't he home yet?'

'I'm not sure. I was on the telephone for some time.'

'He'll be bird-watching.'

'I suppose that's it. Though he's usually ready for his tea.'

Martin brightened. 'Did you say tea? I must say I could use a cup. I've been tinkering with my car for the past two hours.'

'I haven't started tea yet.'

'Well, why don't you? I'll poodle round and look for Simon. He can't be far.'

'Will you? Thanks, Martin. He'll be all right, I know. It's just—'

He smiled. 'It's just an enlarged sense of responsibility – I know. Not to worry, he can't be far. Who's that little scruff he runs around with?'

'Archie Scott? He lives in the cottage next to Jess. I didn't think of that. And Archie's got a new puppy—'

'I'll take a look, then.' Martin lit a cigarette and left at a relaxed pace.

An hour later they had drawn a blank. Grace had had no tea. Martin had swallowed a lukewarm brew and gone to prepare for surgery. Alec had gone direct to the hospital from his afternoon round, so knew nothing of Simon's disappearance.

Once more Grace searched the sloping pastures behind the house. There were so many places which could provide hazards, dark plantations, rocky burns, rough hillsides. He might have fallen and hurt himself in some lonely spot. She called his name, paced the field paths, looked over stone walls, questioned a shepherd, but with no result. A cuckoo called down the vale, mocking her anxiety. There was a hint of dusk in the purple piled clouds to the west. She glanced at her watch. It was nearly surgery time.

Martin met her at the house door. 'No luck?'

'No – and it's nearly surgery time.'

'Not to worry, I can cope. There are not more than six in the waiting-room.'

She hesitated, racked by anxiety. 'Martin, should I call in the police?'

He shrugged. 'Give him another half hour. You know what boys are. And it's still light.'

'But I've just remembered. Isobel warned me – he does wander off sometimes.'

'But he always comes back?'

'Sometimes he has to be brought back.'

'Well, then. Everyone knows him round here. And they'd do anything to oblige Doctor Haydon.'

'I know, but I can't help worrying. I think I'll consult Jess. She might have some ideas—'

The house telephone rang in the hall behind them. Grace ran and snatched up the receiver. 'Lintlaw House!' she gasped.

'Ellis Ridley here,' came a crisp voice. 'Is that Grace Haydon?'

'Yes – what is it?'

'Your young nephew is at this moment in my car. I found him toiling up the road near Thrunton crags. I'm speaking from Hunter's place.'

'Oh, good! I've been so worried.' In that moment of intense relief Grace had almost forgotten the caller's identity. 'You're bringing him back, is that it?'

'Not a bit of it,' was the cool reply. 'I haven't the time. A man is meeting me at Peppercorn to talk business, and I'm late already. I shall take the boy home with me and one of you may drive up and fetch him.'

The reaction from anxiety made her confused. 'But he'll be hungry – and he doesn't know you very well.'

The voice at the end of the line was sarcastic now. 'He's tucking into a hefty sandwich given him by the farmer's wife. And the fact that he doesn't know me well hasn't prevented him from talking non-stop since I picked him up. I may expect someone, then – say within half an hour or so?'

'Yes, about then. Thank you.'

There was a click as he cut her off. She found herself trembling a little. Simon was safe – there was no excuse for this ridiculous urge to cry.

She took a moment to recover, then tapped on the surgery door. Martin appeared, unhooking his stethoscope.

She told him briefly what had happened. 'May I borrow your car? Is it in order?'

He nodded. 'Sure you can manage?'

'Yes. I've driven that model before.'

The evening had turned cold, with a biting east wind and an angry ruffled sunset. She unhooked Simon's duffle coat along with her own.

Only when she was on the road did she realize that now, whether she liked it or not, she must visit Peppercorn again. The realization sent a wave of sick panic through her.

She set her lips and drove steadily, leaving the familiar outlines of the Simonside Hills to the south and heading for the wild country at the head of Coquetdale. Here the road ran along the foothills of the

Cheviots, where sheep grazed unfenced and the young bracken ran rank at the roadside. She passed under the dark shoulders of Kirk Hill and Haugh Law, and a few miles later reached a rough track following a burn, tumbling over its mossy stones to join the river lower down. She swung the car on to the stony surface and began the long bumping climb into the deepening shadows. She remembered now, with vivid intensity, how Douglas had raced down this same track at breakneck pace, each loop and turn a heart-stopping suspense. He had laughed at her nervousness.

'I like to see you frightened, darling. It means I have to console you—'

And when he eventually pulled in there were kisses of blind, aching rapture. . . .

The track slipped down into a hollow, where another smaller burn chattered down its stony channel and flowed across to the opposite side. Now, in dry weather it was little more than a dark stain under the car wheels. Memory stung again. Here she and Douglas had quarrelled. Clear in her mind were the tears she had shed, the heartache of the rift. She strove to remember what had happened.

Yes, she had it now. He had been late picking her up at Lintlaw House, after surgery. When she questioned him he accused her of mistrust. She recalled his chilling anger, which had upset her deeply. Then he had been gentle and contrite, had held her in his arms, here in this lonely hollow, and begged her forgiveness.

'I love you so much, Grace – I can't bear it when you doubt me. I know I get shocking moods and say things I regret afterwards. I even try to hurt you. But it's only because I'm mad at myself.'

Suddenly, too, came memories of other quarrels, of

the aching sweetness of reconciliation. How often he had hurt her, after all, and how often she had forgiven him.

Bewilderment came. Only yesterday she had told herself he was perfect. It had taken this drive over the lonely track to Goatshiels, a road so much a part of their love affair, to unlatch the doors of memory.

No, he had not been perfect, but their tumultuous loving, swinging always between pain and rapture, sun and shadow, had seemed perfect in itself. They had known the heights and the depths together.

'I'll never forget you, Douglas,' she whispered, and the climbing track blurred before her eyes.

She reached a fork; ahead the track climbed to Peppercorn, to the left it wound upwards to that outcrop of isolated rocks, the High Stones of Goatshiels.

Unwillingly her eyes were drawn that way, and cold tension knotted her body. Never again in life, she vowed, would she ever climb that fatal path. It was a relief to turn off through the dark clefts of the hills towards Peppercorn. The track ended at the open stableyard gate. She drove through, turned the car and got out.

Crossing the yard, she cut through a shrubbery and emerged in the sloping walled garden at the front. In the old days she had used the back door, set in the rambling outbuildings abutting on the yard. Today painful instinct urged her to make a more formal entrance; but once in the garden she lingered, overcome by the scene.

Peppercorn stood unchanged as ever, a high-gabled house of the dark local stone, its red pantiles greened over with lichen. It looked squarely to the Cheviots above the glitter of a winding burn. The last flash of the setting sun, still visible at this height, flamed the upstairs windows, and a lazy plume of smoke rose from a chimney. Behind the house, set up the hillside, stood the storm-blown windbreak of dark pines.

The lonely, sturdy grace of the house wrenched at her heart. It had an air of staunch waiting for destiny, of quiet unshaken courage. She thought of the storms it had weathered, the muffling, isolating snows. She remembered golden days when the glory of the heather flowed round it like a grape-purple sea.

Once it had been almost hers. Only yesterday, it seemed, she had laughed and loved within its sturdy walls. Her aching grief rose again to overwhelm her.

She steadied herself, remembering Simon and his need of her. Through the open front door she walked into the hall. Here the sombre gleam of old furniture contrasted with bright handsome rugs. She hesitated, calling Simon's name.

He ran from the dining-room, his small face woebegone. 'Is that you, Auntie Grace? Have you come *already*? I hoped you wouldn't be here for ages yet. We haven't to go now, have we?' He drew her into the room. 'I'm having a super game. Come and see.'

'Are you in here alone? Where's Mr. Ridley?' Anxiety and nervousness sharpened her voice. 'You've been very naughty, Simon.'

His mouth turned down. 'I meant to leave a note, Auntie Grace, honest I did, but I forgot. . . . Mr. Ridley's out in the barn with a man. Look, he lent me this fort and soldiers. He said they used to be his when he was a boy. See, I've got the foot soldiers lined up in the courtyard. These are the enemy cavalry, charging the gates—'

For a moment curiosity took place of annoyance.

She handled one of the soldiers, its paint chipped and faded, visualized a small boy playing alone, banished in disgrace because he refused to call a strange woman 'Mother'. Against her will she was moved, but immediately steeled her heart again.

'We haven't got to go yet, have we?' Simon fretted, his eyes round and anxious under his tumbled rusty hair.

'I'm afraid we must. We can't stay here. Mr. Ridley won't want us.'

'But he said I could play with the soldiers an' I've hardly started.' His face puckered ominously.

'Having trouble?' A decisive voice made her jump. Ellis Ridley stood in the doorway, hunched in an old sweater, his dark face unsmiling.

'Not really. It was very good of you to look after Simon.' Her words were rushed, embarrassed.

He eyed her with leisurely coolness, then walked forward to inspect Simon's battle area.

'H'm . . . the enemy is right in the line of open fire. Not very good generalship. Surely they'd advance on the left flank under cover of the tower?'

'Shall I move them, Mr. Ridley?' Simon deployed his forces afresh.

Ellis Ridley reached out a large brown hand, picked up the general and examined him. His sombre eyes took on a faraway look.

He said quite gently: 'Incidentally, Simon, a general would be directing operations from the fort, not cavorting about like that. He's a very good general. I used to call him Colonel Golightly. That was before he got promotion, of course.'

He turned to Grace with disconcerting suddenness.

'Douglas had an identical set. They're still in the

attic. Perhaps you would like Simon to have them?'

Simon gasped: 'Ooh, please, Auntie Grace.'

She hesitated. 'It's very kind—'

He gave her a quelling glance. 'There's no question of kindness about it. Eventually all Douglas's things will have to go. As I believe you've said yourself, I'm not a sentimental man. I intended to ask you to come over and take away anything you want. But relations have been – strained.'

He seemed to recollect himself, glanced at the sideboard. 'I'm neglecting my duty as host. Will you take a drink, Miss Haydon?'

'No, thank you. I must take Simon home. . . . Er – about Douglas's things – I would like some of his books and photographs. Perhaps some other time.'

She was wretched, longing only to escape. The situation was making severe emotional demands on her. Against this loved interior of Peppercorn, she was seeing again reminders of Douglas in every turn of Ellis Ridley's head, in every glance. And now came this discussion of his possessions, the casting out from his home of the last traces of his life there. Lack of sentiment he might choose to call it, but to her it was the last twist of the knife.

Ellis turned to Simon. 'Pack these up, there's a good lad, and we'll go up and find the other set.' Simon's haste to obey was impressive.

'Do sit down, Miss Haydon,' came the next order. 'Surely you needn't stand on ceremony here, of all places.'

She was glad to obey, her knees assailed by a strange weakness. As the other two mounted to the attics she sat fighting for composure. It would be unthinkable to break down under the critical gaze of Ellis Ridley.

Her gaze cleared, began to take in details of the room. Douglas had been endearingly untidy. In his day the magazine rack had overflowed, the corners were littered with riding-boots, bridles, a gun or two, despite Jess's scolding. Now the room held a certain calm orderliness, the books stacked, the guns marshalled in their rack, even the catalogues and stud-books on the roll-top desk were dust-free. Grace remembered that Billy Middlemass acted as houseman when necessary, but the disciplined comfort of the room was somehow typical of Ellis.

Her roving gaze stilled. On the mantelpiece was a framed photograph of herself with Black Bess.

She got up to look at it. How happy she had been that day. Her laughing face was framed with the mare's in the stable doorway. She had one arm round Bess's neck. And it was Ellis, she remembered, who had taken the photograph. She even recalled how he had walked forward and tucked away a tendril of hair before pressing the trigger.

She retreated in haste to her chair as the others returned. Ellis had noted the movement. 'Are you by any chance coveting that photograph?'

'No. It's just – I'd forgotten about it.'

'It's rather good, I think!' A ghost of a twinkle appeared in his eyes. 'Especially of Bess. She was a lovely mare, too good for Douglas.'

Grace tensed, forcing herself to meet and hold his gaze. 'You soon got rid of her, though, after he died. I suppose you had the chance of a good price?'

'An excellent price.' His dark glance challenged her. 'You used to ride her quite often, I remember. Do you ride much now?'

'No, not at all.' She began to button her coat. As far

as she was concerned, the conversation was over. She was sick and shaken by her own anger.

'It would do you good to have another mount,' he said briskly. 'Nothing like riding. You're too thin and pale. I suppose that brother of yours drives you as hard as he drives himself?'

Grace ignored this and hurried Simon into his duffle coat. 'Thank Mr. Ridley, now, for taking care of you.'

Simon beamed at him. 'Thanks, Mr. Ridley. Thanks for the soldiers too.' He hugged the box. 'It's smashing up here. I'm glad you brought me, even if I didn't find any wild goats.'

'*Wild goats?*' Grace stared at her nephew. 'Simon, is that why you were going to the crags?'

Ellis Ridley put in: 'It seems old Will Robson said something that fired him.'

'Yes, I remember now. I didn't think he would take it so literally.'

'Children usually do.'

Simon gazed up at him. 'Do you think they'll ever come back, Mr. Ridley?'

He smiled. 'Let's just say, if they ever come back to Goatshiels, they'll be welcome. And if that happens, I've already promised to let you know.'

Grace was scarcely listening. She urged Simon to the door. Ellis Ridley reached it first and held it open. 'Don't dissuade him from being a seeker, will you?' he said. 'There's nothing so fascinating as the pursuit of the unattainable.'

His eyes held unreadable depths. At the front door he added: 'I shall be going away for a day or two, quite soon. Perhaps, if I let you know the date later, you would prefer to go through Douglas's things while

I am gone?'

'Thank you. And thank you again for your trouble this afternoon,' she said stiffly.

Simon ran on ahead, and Ellis's gaze went after him. 'He's a promising boy. Don't tread on his dreams too much, will you? Especially now, when he's deprived of his mother. I happen to know just how damaging that can be.'

Again came that unwonted shaft of pity, stealing her composure. He said sharply: 'I imagine you intend to reject my advice, though – just because it *is* mine. Good night, Grace – and take care on the road home.'

He turned a dismissing shoulder and disappeared into the house. As the last rays of the sun sank behind the western hills the darkening contours of the Cheviots seemed to gather brooding about the lonesome house. Grace shivered a little as she turned to follow Simon.

Alec was home when they returned, and Grace was disagreeably surprised by his calm reception of the incident. After scolding Simon for adventuring without permission, he shelved any discussion of the subject until his son was in bed.

Grace was drawing the living-room curtains when Alec said lightly: 'He wasn't a nuisance to Ridley, I hope?'

'He didn't seem to mind.' She spoke curtly. Now that the darkened vale was shut out and she could relax at last in this homely room, she was conscious of a great weariness, the reaction after two hours of emotional pressure.

She sat down and reached for the mending basket.

'Ridley's quite good with children, I believe. Pity

he has none of his own. Simon's taken to him, anyway. He's like a dog with two tails over that set of soldiers.' Alec chuckled over his newspaper.

Grace's ragged nerves reacted. 'I just want you to know, Alec, if Simon ever goes there again, I've no intention of being the one who brings him back,' she flared.

Alec's paper was slowly lowered. He was half amused, half astonished. 'Oh, come on, Gay, what's all this? Isn't it time you got over this stupid antagonism?'

'No, it isn't. And it never will be,' she said wildly. 'Alec, don't you understand—'

Alec was knocking out his pipe in the grate, where a wood fire crackled. 'No, I do not. Really, Grace, get a hold of yourself. What was it, after all? Just a matter of driving there, collecting Simon and exchanging a few courtesies. Even if you didn't mean them, what's so terrible about that?'

'I've told you before, I want no contact with the place.'

'Fair enough. But you'll appreciate that I won't be dictated to about Simon. Naturally I don't want him wandering off, but if he *does* happen to turn up there again, I shall be more than grateful he's in good hands. Peppercorn is scarcely the Bluebeard's Castle you make it out to be, Gay.' His tone was dry.

'It is to me.'

He said firmly: 'We shan't quarrel over this, I hope? And as it's unlikely to happen again anyway, I think we can drop the subject.' He added on a gentler note. 'You look fagged out, Grace. Why don't you have an early night?'

'I think I will.'

From the window of her bedroom she watched the stars over the vale. A soft wind rustled the poplars by the gable. Unwillingly her eyes were drawn westwards, through the darkness towards the hills. What had Ellis Ridley said? 'Don't tread on his dreams—'

She wondered fleetingly what his dream could be. Marriage with Angela, probably.

As for her own dreams, once bright as the milky glitter of these northern stars, they were dead with Douglas. She began to ask herself if she could endure to stay here until Isobel's recovery. It was all so much harder than she had expected.

Yet Alec and Simon needed her. There could be no going back. She drew the curtains against the stars.

Before long Grace felt she had never been away from Abbotshaws. Gradually her doubts and depressions faded. It was impossible to be despondent while Isobel improved daily, while Simon ran bounding with health in the daisied pastures.

She watched the signs of the march of the year with growing happiness. As May wore into June, with squalls of rain and brilliant spells of sun, the broom, the gorse and the may coloured the hedgerows. In the woods behind the church bluebells spread like an inland sea, and arching spines of dog-roses showed tightly folded buds. She saw the corn on the valley floor thicken to a blinding green, saw the lambs flourish and fatten on the hill pastures. It was the slack times of the sheep-farmers' year, before the dipping and shearing.

At the surgery there was a notable thinning of surgeries, a shrinking of rounds. At the Whitsun holiday Martin was able to plan a week-end in London, as

Alec cancelled the Monday surgery.

He was ready to leave after breakfast on Saturday morning. Jess waylaid him in the hall with a packed lunch and two thermos flasks.

'At least I'll know you've had a good start, Doctor Finch. For when you get there you'll be eating all kinds of rubbish, I'll be bound!' she said.

Martin winked at Grace. 'You're dead right, Jess. No home-baked singing hinnies down there. I'll be eating frogs' legs and birds'-nest soup.... Where do you think London is, anyway? In the Far East?'

'I know fine where it is – down *south*!' The contempt in Jess's voice set them both laughing.

'Don't tell me you've never been to London, Jess?'

'I have *not*, Doctor Finch. I'm no' likely to be gallivanting that distance. I've heard it's a right fine place, though. And I wouldn't say no to seeing Buckingham Palace and the Tower of London, not to mention Westminster Abbey. You'll be going all round those places this week-end, I suppose?'

'You bet your life,' Martin assured her gravely. 'And if I work all three in tomorrow that'll leave Monday for Hampton Court, Hyde Park Corner, Kew Gardens and the Zoo.'

Grace's eyes danced. Jess regarded him dourly. 'Aye, I know you're laughing at me, Doctor Finch. I'm no' as green as I'm cabbage-looking, either!'

Alec had arrived on the scene. He said coolly, after an eyebrow raised at Martin: 'I seem to remember a certain young man who thought we all wore skins, burned peat and slept in the pens with the sheep. Or something very near it!'

Martin grinned, a little abashed. 'Yes, well, we live and learn.... Never mind, Jess, I'll bring you back a postcard of Buckingham Palace as big as one of your plate-pies.'

Grace walked with him to the car. 'Give my love to London, Martin. I can feel quite sentimental about it now. While I was there I just felt trapped.'

'Ah, but it's the best trap in the world!' Martin hesitated, his eyes softening. 'Will you miss me?'

She smiled. 'Of course I will. It's been fun, having someone young to talk to. Think of me tonight having strangulated hernias over the supper table.'

'I'll think of you all. . . . This is the life, when all's said and done. I'm beginning to wonder if I'll ever go back permanently to the rat-race.'

'I knew it would get you in the end,' she teased.

He slung his bag in the back of the estate car. 'I nearly forgot to ask you – if I get tickets for the Young Farmers' Ball, will you come as my partner?'

She was startled.

'Please!' Martin begged. 'I hear it's quite an occasion.'

'Oh, it is! Yes, I'd like to, thanks.'

He beamed. 'Then it's a date.' He reached out and squeezed her hand. 'See you Monday night!'

She watched him drive away, conscious of a prick of loss. More than anyone, he had helped her through black days, just by being his relaxed cheerful self.

She heard Jess's voice at her elbow. 'Aye, he's a canny lad, is Doctor Finch. You could go further and fare worse, Miss Haydon. He'd make a canny husband.' She smoothed her white apron.

Grace stiffened. 'I'm not looking for a husband, Jess.'

Jess eyed her shrewdly. 'You'll get over Douglas. No' yet, maybe, but in time. You canna live on sorrow for ever. And I'll say this – Doctor Finch likes you. Miss Angela fancied him before you arrived, but she's chasing Mr. Ridley now. And I'm feared he'll be dazzled by her looks, for she's no' good enough for him.'

'I think they're very well matched!' Grace said coldly.

'Aye, well, you've still a grudge against Mr. Ridley.' Jess added ironically: 'It's as well we're both quiet bodies, or we might have to come to words on that score.'

'There'll be no danger of that, Jess – if you'll kindly not mention Ellis Ridley's name to me.'

Jess flushed with indignation. 'I've told you before, Miss Haydon, he was a good master to me. And with all respects to you, I'll no' have him miscalled. I know you thought Mr. Douglas was perfect, but I could tell you a thing or two—'

'I'm sure you could, Jess! I happen to know you'd believe anything Ellis Ridley liked to tell you. And it's a habit of his to speak slightingly of Douglas – now he's gone and can't answer back!'

She trembled before the force of her own anger, sick with despair that her relaxed happiness of a moment ago should be destroyed by mention of Ellis Ridley.

Jess grew subdued. 'I'll say no more, Miss Haydon. I've been forgetting my place, and that's not like me. Did you mean to keep that cold meat for supper to-night?'

Grace replied quietly, and the incident passed. But she was appalled at the depth of her disturbance and angry at Jess's blindness. Once again she asked herself how everyone could be so deceived, why she alone could see Ellis Ridley in true perspective.

CHAPTER FOUR

THAT weekend Grace missed Martin about the place, but the thought of the Young Farmers' Ball brought pleasant anticipation. After tucking Simon up in bed on the Sunday evening she went to her own room to decide about a suitable dress.

When she had left Abbotshaws for London she had taken few clothes with her. The rest Isobel had stored for her. In the darkest corner of the fitted cupboard, pushed to the end of the rail, were several dresses belonging to the period of her engagement. She unhooked them, stripped off the polythene covers and spread them on the bed.

Memories swooped and tore. This gold chiffon – she had danced in it all night at a twenty-first birthday party over at Bellingham. That was the night Douglas proposed. The green velvet sheath brought Christmas to mind, the tree and presents at home with the family, then Douglas calling with the car to drive her through the frost-rimed hills to Peppercorn. Ellis had friends staying and the small gathering became a party. Douglas kissed her under the mistletoe, and then Ellis.

She stood motionless, the folds of the dress in her hands. The scene flashed vividly into her mind. Yes, Ellis had elbowed Douglas aside and demanded his turn. And now with sickening clarity she remembered his kiss. That of Douglas she could not recall, but again came the sensation of Ellis's strong arms about her, his dark unsmiling face and the firm cool kiss. She remembered something else, too, and rooted in a dress-ing-table drawer for a small box.

This was Ellis's Christmas present, given almost casually later in the evening; an antique bracelet set with aquamarines.

'It hasn't any great value,' he told her. 'But it's a pretty thing and belonged to my mother. An aunt recently left it to me along with other family trifles. And as the new bride of Peppercorn I would like you to have it.'

She had been all delight and gratitude. Now she examined it with reluctance. She would never wear it now. Yet she remembered with pity that young Welsh bride who had been his mother, dying while still a young woman.

She stowed the box away, unwilling to keep it, but with the feeling that she had no right to dispose of it. She turned again to the dresses, and fingered one of a forget-me-not blue lace, cut low at the neck. Of all her late-day dresses it was her favourite, and of a dateless style.

These clothes could not be kept in mothballs for ever, she decided. This one especially had been associated with happiness, not sorrow. To wear it again might bring a shadow of old delight. And it was a perfect foil for her hair.

With it she had always worn the aquamarine bracelet. It was exactly the right colour. But not this time. Ellis Ridley must not have the satisfaction of seeing it on her arm. And he was almost certain to be at the Ball, as a past Chairman of the committee.

She tried on the dress. It needed taking up an inch, but she found with a shock that it hung loosely about her waist. And because she saw now in the mirror only a slender ghost of that other shapely self, tears gathered and blinded her.

What had Angela said? 'Her looks have quite gone.'

She hoped it might not be quite true. She wanted to look her best for Martin, because he was a strength and a comfort to her. It was too soon to decide if he would ever be anything more.

Alec was pleased to hear of the planned outing, and had told Isobel all about it. She sent her love and the offer of her own evening wrap if needed. Peggy's services were booked in good time for sitting-in.

On Monday evening Martin returned, full of his weekend but delighted to be back. He greeted Grace warmly, and anxiously reminded her of their date.

'Don't worry,' she smiled. 'Everything's arranged.'

The Ball was on the following Saturday, and was held in a large hotel on the Newcastle side of Rothbury. They stopped in the town for a drink before driving the last few miles.

'We must get in the mood,' he assured her. 'I can't think of anything worse than doing the cha-cha-cha in cold blood.'

Grace laughed. Already anticipation lent a new sparkle to her eyes. They found a quiet nook in a lounge bar and Martin ordered drinks. He looked gay and relaxed in formal clothes, his fairness accentuated by the dark cloth. She noticed envious glances from other women and realized how attractive Martin really was.

He studied her, his head on one side. 'You look wonderful, Grace. That blue is sheer genius with your hair and eyes.' He added softly: 'I've been looking forward to this all the time I was away. Believe it or not, I was scared to ask you. Those first weeks after you came I thought you'd retreated from the world, like a nun.'

Grace coloured. 'Martin! Was I as bad as all that?'

'You were withdrawn. You reminded me of a rose left out in the frost, still flowering but only held together by ice.'

'And now?'

'Now you're thawing.' He covered her hand with his. 'You really went overboard for Douglas Ridley, didn't you?'

She nodded, biting her lip.

'And still do?'

'I love his memory and always shall. If he'd died in a normal way I might have resigned myself. But an accident always seems tragic and senseless. I keep asking myself why it had to happen.'

'Doctors ask themselves these things too.' He was serious now. 'But we don't find the answers and we can't brood about it. There are always other people needing us.'

She met his eyes steadily. 'Is that a message – for me?'

'Why not? You can't make Douglas happy. He's beyond all that. But there's young Doctor Finch—' he imitated the local accent – 'A right canny lad, fair gasping for a bit of notice.'

She laughed. 'I'll do my best.'

'You're doing fine. Let's have another drink, then we can make a late entrance and knock 'em all cold!'

The late entrance, to her relief, was made during a crowded dance number, and by the time the band ceased playing they were installed at a table beside the floor, able to relax and enjoy the scene.

The room was panelled in Regency style, with a handsome ceiling. Flowers were massed before the band platform. The guests were a true cross-section of local society, from the Master of the hunt down to teenage farmers' sons from the in-bye sheep holdings.

At some distance from their own table sat Ellis Ridley with Angela, a breathtaking figure in an exotic cyclamen sheath. Grace saw and stiffened. Martin gave a wry smile.

'Ah, my old flame! She seems to mean business with Ridley, doesn't she?'

'I think it's mutual.'

Grace was uneasy. Ellis Ridley's gaze had unerringly sought her out, and he was staring most pointedly. Then the band struck up another number and she was safe in Martin's arms and swaying in a waltz, oblivious of everything but the pleasure of the moment.

Martin held her just a little closer than a casual partner might. She gave herself up to the rhythm, relaxing in a dreamy acceptance of delight.

During the next hour she met many old friends, young people who had known Douglas well. She introduced Martin. ... 'Bill Adams, Jack and Linda. ... The Dixons – Nell, Oliver, David ...'

They were warmly welcoming, gracefully tactful concerning the past; almost too tactful sometimes, walking on tip-toe through an ambush of pitfalls. She felt the strain and after a while excused herself to repair her make-up.

When she got back to the floor she saw Martin approach Angela and ask for a dance. They swung into a spirited quickstep, seemed to be having an animated conversation. She was just about to sit down when a voice came from behind:

'Would you care to dance, Miss Haydon?'

She turned to find Ellis Ridley waiting, an obvious challenge in his eyes.

Grace was dumbstruck. This was a possibility she ought to have foreseen. He waited with ironic patience for her answer, yet she could find none. It was an impossible situation. She could neither bring herself to dance with him nor to refuse, a breach of manners needing an impeccable excuse. And she was sorely aware that people were watching.

'I'm surprised you should ask me,' she stalled.

His dark brows drew together. 'I can't imagine why. Your partner is dancing with mine. It would be poor courtesy to leave you sitting alone.' He hesitated, then said caustically: 'Don't worry, Grace. I don't usually inflict myself on women who detest me. Perhaps you will allow me to bring you a drink, and then I promise to leave you in peace.' He indicated her glass. 'What was it?'

'Gin and french, thank you.'

She sat down, curiously weak at the knees, and with the wretched knowledge that she had behaved badly.

Angry tears pricked her eyes. Why had he approached her, when he must know his presence was an embarrassment? Did he hope to wipe out that past debt by a display of his forceful charm? Did he really rate her intelligence so low?

He set the drink before her and sat down. She thanked him and a tense silence came. Dancing couples cast them curious glances and plainly gossiped. Everyone knew the shadow between them, and Grace was acutely conscious of being on view, like a butterfly in a glass case, pinned down for inspection.

At last he leaned towards her and said: 'I remember that dress. You used to wear the aquamarine bracelet with it.'

'Yes.'

'But not any more?'

She flushed. 'I'm wearing a necklace instead.'

'So I see,' he said drily.

Their eyes met briefly, hers defiant, his narrowed and reflective. 'You've lost weight, Grace.'

She sat in silence, suffering his stare, praying for the dance to end. He offered her a cigarette. She shook her head.

'So even tonight the barriers are up? Can't you bring yourself to pretend a little?'

'Why should I?'

'Perhaps because we are very much on view. Why give the tittle-tattlers more ammunition?'

'*I* have no reason to be afraid of them.'

Those stormy grey eyes were intimidating now. Her heart missed a beat, moved on jerkily. 'Poor Grace,' he said softly. 'Nothing left but your pride – oh, and of course young Lochinvar, even now glowering in my direction!'

She realized the band had stopped playing, the dancers were dispersing. As Martin and Angela joined them, Ellis got to his feet.

Angela slid her arm in his, demanding a drink in cool ringing tones; but her gaze swept speculatively over Grace.

Martin set a possessive hand on Grace's shoulder. 'All right?' he asked softly.

The two men eyed each other. Ellis gave Grace a cool nod. 'Excuse me.' He steered Angela towards the bar.

Martin watched their retreating backs. 'They make a handsome couple, don't they?' he said lightly. Then: 'Has Ridley been annoying you?' He sat down and reached for his glass.

She forced a smile. 'Not exactly. I could have done without his company, though ... Angela's a good dancer, isn't she?'

He nodded. '*And* a good actress. I was subjected to a lot of false vivacity, produced with the sole intention of making Ridley jealous. Pity he was too busy looking at you.'

'You sound upset, Martin.'

'I can't stand the man, that's all.' He raised his glass. 'Let's forget them, shall we? Here's to us ... And listen to that cha-cha-cha! Come and cut a rug!' Smiling, he drew her to her feet.

They danced together for the next hour. Gradually she relaxed again, trying not to be so conscious of Ellis Ridley's tall figure looming at intervals, that breathtaking likeness to Douglas, reminding her of other nights, other dances, in the far, glamorous past.

Later, as they sat at their table, a waiter approached. 'Doctor Finch?' Martin nodded. 'A telephone call for you, sir.'

Martin grimaced. 'Keep your fingers crossed. It may be an emergency.'

He returned in haste. 'Sorry, Grace, it just had to happen, I suppose. That was Doctor Haydon. He's had two emergency calls within five minutes. I'll have to attend the one nearest here – it's over Snitter way. Thank heaven my bag's in the car.'

She rose. 'I'll get my coat.'

'Can't you stay and get a lift home? I may be detained some time. It's a baby case. What about the Adamses? Couldn't they take you?'

'I suppose so. But I don't really want to stay.' She knew a helpless inability to explain. Without Martin she felt so emotionally exposed. There were friends she could join, parties who would welcome her at their tables, but the rift of time and their too careful tact would make conversation painful.

'Just go,' she urged. It was unfair to keep him waiting while she dithered. 'I'll get a lift all right.'

'Sure? I hate to leave you like this,' he fretted.

She gave him a gentle push. 'I'm not a doctor's sister for nothing!'

'I'm sorry,' he said again, and was gone. Alone, she reached a quick decision.

Her feeling of vulnerability was now stronger and increased at every glimpse of Ellis Ridley. She hurried to the cloakroom, collected her coat, then found a quiet corner of the entrance lounge near the main door. She occupied herself with a pile of magazines, meaning to beg a lift from any early leavers whom she knew might be driving towards Abbotshaws.

Soon she was yawning and weary, yet she knew this was due to disappointment and a sense of anti-climax rather than any physical cause. It could have been a most successful evening. Martin was so very much her kind of person. Though he had none of her shyness and reticence, he had a certain sensitivity that divined her every mood. Bracingly teasing one moment, he could be quietly understanding the next. She remembered Jess's advice. Yes, Martin would make a good husband. But marriage needed more than good husbands and good wives. There had to be fire rather than mere warmth, the spark ignited by the attraction of opposites.

Without warning she was swamped again in a black wave of bitterness, of painful wild longing for Douglas.

A voice roused her. 'Anything wrong, Grace?'

She looked up into the blunt freckled face of Jack

Adams, Douglas's one-time friend.

'Oh, sorry, Jack! I was dreaming.'

'I heard Doctor Finch was called away. Are you all right for a lift?'

She shook her head, smiling. 'That's why I'm here, hoping to waylay someone going Abbotshaws way.'

'Come with us, then. We're leaving almost right away – going on to a party at Glanton.'

'Devils for punishment, aren't you?'

He grinned. 'You know how it is. Seems tame to go straight home. Remember how Douglas—' His voice snapped off. His face flushed a dull red under his sandy hair. 'Yes, well, I'll just go and round them up.'

She sighed, relieved that her problem was solved, a little upset because Jack had clumsily tried to save her feelings. If only people would be more natural! How could she ever recover if no one would discuss Douglas calmly?

Five minutes later a small crowd spilled out of the ballroom; Jack and his brother Bill, his sister Helen and two other girls. She rose to slip on her coat. Next moment she saw Ellis Ridley behind them, head and shoulders taller than the stocky Adams boys. Angela was at his side.

Jack joined Grace. 'I'm sorry, I didn't know our Helen had already offered Belle Marshall a lift. That's our car to bursting point. But I've got you fixed up. Mr. Ridley's taking you. Suits us better as he has to go to Abbotshaws anyway, with Miss Forster. And we can cut through by New Moor. Good night!'

She had no time to argue or protest. The Adams contingent swept on, calling cheerful farewells, and she was left facing Ellis Ridley and an affronted Angela.

'It doesn't matter,' she stammered. 'I'll ask someone else. I didn't know Jack—'

'Don't distress yourself,' he broke in drily. 'You may as well come with us. And as young Adams realized, we're probably the only ones going your way.'

'Aren't you lucky?' Angela shrugged. 'I don't even mind you playing gooseberry!'

Her tone implied that in Grace Haydon there could be no serious competition. She went on: 'You look tired, sweetie. Too bad you had to lose your escort, wasn't it?'

Grace stood silent and humiliated, feeling a nuisance, wanting wildly to get out of this situation; but there was something final about Ellis Ridley's sharp rejoinder.

'I imagine Finch was needed urgently. With the medical profession, duty comes first, and very rightly so. I'll bring the car round.'

He left them. She waited in miserable resignation, longing only for the journey to be over.

'Cigarette?' Angela flourished a gold case. 'No? Too bad Martin had to go, wasn't it? I suppose it really *was* an emergency? From all I hear he has various interests in the district.' She laughed softly.

Grace set her lips and refused to be goaded.

'We don't like to be teased, do we?' Angela blew a cloud of smoke in her face. 'You know me – I just can't resist it.'

'Yes, I know you, Angela. You haven't changed a bit.'

She remembered a scene in the school playground, when Angela had deliberately torn the wings from a live butterfly; recalled too her own furious attack, the sound of her voice raised in blazing protest. Now she felt as vulnerable as that poor insect, but without the heart to fight.

'There's the car!' Angela stalked ahead on elegant slender legs, her dress glowing like a jewel in the moonlight. Grace slid into the rear seat. Throughout the drive home she was ignored, while Angela gave an amused commentary on the dance.

Ellis Ridley answered only in monosyllables, seeming intent on his driving. At Abbotshaws he swung the car into the drive of the Grange. Angela stopped talking in mid-sentence. 'No, Ellis, it should be Lintlaw House first to drop Grace. You know you said you'd come in for a drink.'

He sent the car hurtling up the long incline between the crowding pines. 'I intended to, yes. But since then I've found I have to go up to Newcastle early in the morning.'

'On a Sunday?' Angela's voice was querulous. 'Horses again, I suppose.'

'As you say – horses again.' The car grated to a halt on the gravel. He got out, walked with Angela towards the pillared entrance of the Grange. In a moment they were lost in shadow. Grace wondered if they were kissing. She remembered again that kiss under the mistletoe. Was it like that with Angela, firm and cool and demanding ... She shook herself. What could it matter to her? She found herself dreading the next part of the journey, when she would be alone with him.

Ellis Ridley's tall figure loomed out of the darkness. He drove in silence down the drive and up the village street. At Lintlaw House the light burned over the front door, as always, a beacon of healing to the vale. He backed the car into the open driveway and pulled up facing his return road. Grace was already fumbling at the door. He got out and whipped it open unexpectedly. She lost her balance, found herself caught in his arms and set on her feet.

'Steady! And I don't think it could be all those gins and french. You could scarcely be called a hardened tippler.'

His tone was mildly amused, but his hands still held her. He stood between her and the blessed sanctuary of home. He blotted out the light of healing. Pinned by his hold, she panicked.

'Please let me go.' He laughed gently, tightening his grasp.

'Take your hands off me!' she flared. He released her.

'You really do hate me, don't you? You can't bear me to touch you.' His voice was a lash. 'To you I'm a kind of leper. Perhaps you would like me to wear a bell and go about crying: "Unclean, unclean!" '

Without warning he seized her again. 'Seems I might as well be hanged for a sheep as a lamb.' He jerked her into his embrace, kissed her deliberately and without mercy, then pushed her away.

'Now you can really have it in for me, my dear!'

He slammed into the car, let in the clutch, and roared away up the vale road towards the hills.

Grace stood motionless, a hand to her mouth. The imprint of that kiss smarted and burned like a brand. She was outraged, bewildered, stung to a raw new life.

That kiss had held all of Douglas's passion, but with a darker mastery. There had even been a brief moment of loss and loneliness when he thrust her away.

Trembling, she admitted this, but surely her reactions had been purely automatic? Her senses had responded because this was how his brother's kisses had once roused her.

She let herself in, spoke a few words to Peggy Everitt, and walked with the girl to her cottage gate. Only when she was alone in her bedroom did deeper feelings displace the first effects of shock.

That kiss was typical of the man. He had admitted to being beyond her respect, and then proceeded to prove it. Later he would no doubt share his callous amusement with Angela. Helpless anger seared her. There seemed no way of avoiding him. Now he had imprinted on her an unforgettable incident. Each time she saw him she would be humiliated afresh. . . .

She slept badly that night. Restless torment of mind brought strange confused dreams, periods of wakefulness while the stars paled and the dawn showed grey at the window. The piping sweetness of the bird chorus aroused her at last. She remembered with relief that it was Sunday, the easiest of her days.

Martin slept late, as he had been long hours on his baby case. She walked as usual with Alec and Simon to the village church.

During the singing of the psalm, she felt Simon nudge her sharply. She looked down. His face was ablaze with excitement. His podgy finger traced the words of the next verse:

'The high hills are a refuge for the wild goats
And the rocks for the conies –'

She smiled at him, touched by his transparent happiness. The imagination of a child was such a precious gift. Simon carried his dream of the goats wherever he went, secure against all adult scepticism. Strange how Ellis Ridley had accepted that dream in all seriousness, he who had no feeling for animals. The man was an impossible enigma.

Last night's kiss seemed now a strange mad dream. Flushing, she bent her face over the prayer-book, conscious of Alec's staid solidity beside her. What would *he* think if he knew? And Isobel . . . And Martin?

That Martin was jealous of Ellis Ridley had been made plain at the Ball. Yet the thought roused no excitement, only a wan pity. Martin deserved better than a second-hand heart.

After the service Simon begged leave to play with Archie Scott until lunch-time. It was a chill morning, a sharp east wind stripping the flowerets from the candles of horse-chestnut by the lych gate. Heavy, driving clouds obscured the sun. Not the best of days for wading in the cold waters of the village burn, but this the two boys did, Simon arriving home sneezing and wet to the waist after losing his footing in the water.

By nightfall he had developed a feverish cold. On Monday Grace had a small patient to nurse upstairs besides all her household and surgery duties. Alec prescribed for his son, considered the infection nothing serious and left him to her care. Lying in bed too restless to read, he began unexpectedly to fret for his mother.

'I wish Mummy was here.' He turned tearful eyes to her face. 'Wouldn't they let her out of hospital just to see me?'

Grace tucked him up for the twentieth time. 'I'm afraid not, darling.'

'You'd think they'd let ladies come and see their boys, wouldn't you?'

'It's just not possible – Mummy's not well enough. Why not turn over and try to sleep?'

He ignored that, his eyes fixed and anxious. 'She is there, isn't she? In the hospital?'

'Of course she is.'

'You wouldn't tell a lie – cross your heart and hope to die?'

For his comfort she repeated his words. 'What *is* all this, darling?'

Simon's next words made her heart turn over.

'Archie Scott says she's dead!'

'Simon!'

'He says you're all scared to tell me. He said his Mum told him his granddad had gone away to hospital and he found out it was a lie. His granddad was dead all the time!' Again the perplexed, panic-stricken look.

She hugged him. 'Oh, darling, what nonsense! Why, your mummy wrote you a note only the other day.'

'Archie Scott says you could have forged it.'

'Archie Scott is very naughty! As if we would do a thing like that! Would you like Daddy to come and talk to you when he gets back?'

'No, I want to see Mummy. I want to see her so I'll know she's still there.' He buried his face in the pillow.

Grace strove to console him, but with little success. When Alec returned from his morning round she followed him into the surgery and told him what had happened.

He frowned. 'This is bad. Not unusual in a feverish child, of course.' He perched on his desk, ruminating. 'Have you any ideas, Gay? Beyond wringing young Archie's neck, of course!'

'Not really, unless ... You're going to the hospital tonight. I suppose Isobel couldn't speak to him on the bedside telephone?'

'You've forgotten something, haven't you? It means she'll have to know he's ill, and then she's going to start worrying.'

He lapsed into further thought. 'Wait a minute – I've got it. Isobel's allowed out of bed now. She can get to the ward window. As soon as Simon's temperature's down I'll take him to the hospital and he can wave to her from the grounds. That way she won't suspect anything is wrong.'

Grace smiled, all relief. 'When do you think he'll be fit enough?'

'A couple of days. That is if this absurd idea doesn't give him a setback.'

Martin looked in, saw their serious faces and asked what the trouble was. When Grace explained Martin said: 'Shall I go and chat him up? I could start with birds and animals and then mention casually that I'd seen his mother at the hospital.'

Alec shrugged. 'It might work. Thanks.'

Through the open surgery door they watched him take the stairs two at a time. 'He's a good chap, isn't he?' Alec smiled. 'I thought he was on the casual side at first, but we live and learn. He's very fond of you, Grace.'

'Is he?' She coloured.

Alex said quietly: 'You might do worse, you know.'

'There's nothing like that, Alec. It's too soon.'

He gazed at her reflectively. 'I was hoping you'd begun to get over that other business. Pity Ridley had to come back. I suppose continually seeing him around doesn't help. That reminds me – I heard some news on my rounds. I'd a call to make at Longheugh. Ralph Muckle has fibrositis. He tells me Ridley is buying that old breeding stud near Rothbury. The sale doesn't include the house, so he plans to dig in for good at Peppercorn and run it from there.'

'I heard he was looking for a place.' She tried to sound unconcerned. Next moment Martin came downstairs, despondent.

'Sorry. I couldn't get him to listen at all.'

'Not to worry,' Alec reassured him. 'I'll try a sedative. A few hours' sound sleep might improve the situation.'

At the doorway he turned. 'Oh, and Gay, while he's well out I insist you get a rest yourself. You've been run off your feet.' He collected some tablets from the dispensary and went upstairs.

Grace and Martin were silent for a moment.

'Bad luck,' he said at last. 'But I can understand it. When I was a kid I used to imagine the most frightful things. And young Archie probably got a kick out of scaring him. Boys can be devils that way.'

Grace nodded. 'I hope he doesn't get worse. It would be dreadful having to lie to Isobel, but we can't have her worrying. It might mean a bad setback.'

'Don't cross your bridges—' he warned her. 'By the way, how did you enjoy Saturday night, or rather what we had of it?'

'It was wonderful,' she smiled.

'Who took you home?'

'Ellis Ridley.' Her voice sounded self-conscious.

Martin turned his back to flip through a medical magazine. She sensed his annoyance. 'I thought he was toting Angela Forster?'

'He was. I played gooseberry in the back seat.' She spoke lightly. 'I'd rather have had a lift from anyone else, of course, but I got talked into it by the Adamses. It meant saving them a detour.'

Martin faced her again. 'I was disappointed. Duty called and all that, but it did spoil the evening. You will come out with me again?'

'I'd like to.'

He relaxed into a smile. 'Good – we could run over to Newcastle for a dinner-dance. When Simon's better, of course. You'll be ready for a spot of relaxation then.'

Jess walked into the hall to sound the lunch-gong. Grace called: 'Better leave it, Jess, Doctor Haydon's trying to settle Simon down to sleep.'

'Right you are, Miss Haydon. Did you no' see your letter? The post's been. It's here on the hall table.'

Grace picked up the square envelope. The handwriting was unfamiliar, a black spiky scrawl. As Martin passed her to go to the dining-room she glanced up, saw Jess's gaze fixed on the letter, perplexed.

She turned away reluctantly. 'I'll serve up now, then.'

Grace scanned the single sheet of notepaper and saw the bold flourish of Ellis Ridley's signature. Her heart raced uncomfortably.

'Dear Miss Haydon,' she read: 'Please try to forget my behaviour on Saturday night, the result of having drunk too much. I can promise you it will not happen again. This is to say I shall be going away tomorrow for a couple of days. It might suit you to collect any of Douglas's things from Peppercorn during my absence. Billy Middlemass is usually about and will let you in. Yours, Ellis Ridley.'

She thrust the letter into her cardigan pocket. Jess appeared with the soup tureen and gave her a sharp scrutiny. It was obvious she knew the handwriting and wondered what was afoot.

Alec came down, announced that Simon was quiet and drowsy. Lunch passed normally. As usual Grace went to help Jess with the washing-up.

They worked in silence for a while. Jess clashed the plates loudly and at last remarked: 'I suppose you've heard Mr. Ridley is buying another place?'

'A breeding stud, isn't it?'

'Ay. He's wanted that one for some time. Folks are saying he's thinking of getting wed into the bargain!'

She glanced dourly at Grace, waiting for her reply.

'I suppose he will, eventually.' She tried to speak evenly. 'Angela Forster seems pretty sure about it, anyway.'

'It wouldn't be the first time a lass made plans in his direction, but he'll take some pinning down. For all *she* knows he might be playing her up.' Again her glance plainly asked a question.

Grace carefully dried a coffee cup. 'Knowing Ellis Ridley, I wouldn't be surprised.'

Jess hesitated, dish-mop poised. She said quietly: 'I saw the letter, Miss Haydon, and I knew the writing. It set me wondering, that's all.' She gave Grace a sharp scrutiny. 'You'll forgive an older woman's curiosity? All I'm concerned about is Mr. Ridley's happiness.'

Grace shrugged. 'Why, Jess, the letter was nothing. Just some business concerning Douglas. I'm to have some of his things from Peppercorn, that's all. Surely you didn't think—'

Jess bent lower over the sink. 'I know you're set against him. That's why I got a shock, like – knowing he was writing to you. And if I thought out of turn, then I'm sorry.'

She washed some cutlery, stood it in a jug to drain, and went on:

'It's maybe hard for a lassie like you to understand, but Mr. Ridley might have been my own son, I set such store by him. To my mind he hasn't met a lass yet fit to be his wife. Yon Angela Forster's as hard as Scotch granite. And I'd hate to see him take another man's leavings. He needs a good quiet unselfish lass, one who'll give him her first love, the love he's gone short of all his life. ... Aye, but I doubt he'll never find her. He's ower proud and particular, is Mr. Ridley.'

Grace knew a hot resentment. 'Everyone doesn't think as you do, Jess. He may have been kind and considerate to you, but—'

'A kinder master never breathed!'

'We all speak from experience, though. And you know mine.' Grace hung up the tea-towel. Jess's former words flared in her mind: 'Another man's leavings – a lass who'll give him her first love—'

Was Jess actually warning her off? She might have been furious if the insinuation had been less ridiculous.

Yet she left the kitchen with a new understanding of the older woman. It was clear now that she had tried to mother Ellis and considered herself in a position to criticize his choice. Poor Jess, so dour yet so sentimental, so devoted yet so deceived. It was almost incredible that she should still believe Ellis Ridley to be a good man.

Within a few hours, however, she had totally forgotten the incident. Towards evening it became evident that Simon was worse. His temperature had risen and Alec began to speak of the possibility of pneumonia.

CHAPTER FIVE

'WHAT about telling Isobel now?' Grace asked in a low voice. She sat in a chair by Simon's bedside, drained of all strength by the demands of the past night.

Alec softly paced the room, shaking his head. Two days had passed and his fears were justified. A sputum test had revealed the causal organism to be broncho-pneumonia, and he had begun treatment at once. If no complications came the infection should be arrested within three days by the antibiotic. For all that, she knew he was still worried.

'We won't tell her yet,' he said. His blunt, kindly face was stern with tension. 'It's a hell of a decision, though. And if Isobel knew I was withholding this she'd be furious. But I've got to consider her position too.'

'You're not really expecting complications, are you?'

He shook his head, but doubt lingered in his eyes. 'I can't overdo the sedatives, you know. And if he continues to fret about his mother it could well set him back.'

'He might have forgotten by the time he wakes.' She turned to smooth the damp tousled hair from Simon's brow.

'We can only hope he has. . . . It's the visiting that worries me.'

Last evening Alec had missed his usual visit to his wife. Martin, who was in on the pitiful little conspiracy, had telephoned the ward sister to say Alec had been detained over an emergency case, which was only too sadly true. There still remained other evenings.

'The trouble is, I'm just no use at putting on an act,' Alec mused. 'One look at my face and Isobel would know immediately something was wrong. What about you, Gay? Women make better deceivers than men.'

'I'll go if you want me to. One visit would be all right, but surely if I went twice she would smell a rat?'

Alec's heavy shoulders heaved in a sigh. 'We'll just have to play it as it comes, then.' He yawned and made for the door. 'I'll take a bath and make some coffee.'

They had shared the night's vigil. Having slept uneasily for a couple of hours, Grace now moved quietly about the room, setting it tidy for the coming day. It was not yet seven o'clock, and a heavy sullen dawn had only just begun to brighten, a gusty breeze tossing the elms behind the stable-yard. For the past two days Grace had been virtually a prisoner in the house.

Later that morning, as the sedative wore off, Simon moved restlessly and began to cough again. He opened his eyes and whimpered, 'Mummy, are you there?'

Grace noted with alarm the sudden bluish appearance of his skin. She ran down for Alec, who had not yet begun surgery. He examined his son with a grave face. 'He's already cyanosed and needs oxygen.'

A supply of oxygen, with disposable plastic masks, was kept in the surgery. The treatment brought some relief but worried the child.

'All right, old man. Just pretend it's a space helmet. There now, you can breathe better, can't you?'

Grace sat holding Simon's hand. There could be no question of leaving Simon unattended, and the household arrangements needed urgent consideration. Jess came up to announce that she had found a neighbour to cook for her father and could stay the whole day.

'That'll save you worry over the meals, Miss Haydon, and I can maybe take over by the wee laddie while you get the odd rest.'

'It's very good of you, Jess.' Grace managed an exhausted smile. 'Doctor Finch is doing both rounds so that Alec can stay. Thank heaven there's no evening surgery today. But I shall have to go to Newcastle tonight to visit Isobel.'

'You'll never do it, my lassie!'

'I've got to,' Grace protested.

Simon worsened. Despite the oxygen he became so exhausted by toxic delirium that Alec gave an intramuscular injection of paraldehyde. As the day wore on, sad with sagging clouds and driving squalls of rain, Simon cried out feverishly for his mother. Between the intervals of taking oxygen he rambled about his guinea-pigs, the wild goats, even about Douglas.

'I won't tell, Douglas, I promise. Only get me a magpie to tame. You said you would. Please, Douglas—'

Grace's blood ran cold. What old incident was this?

'Please, Douglas, you know I always wanted a magpie—'

She stroked his head. 'Hush, darling!'

'Mummy, I'm hot. I want Mummy.' His hand clasped her hotly. Gradually her head drooped to the pillow beside his. She dozed and awoke with a shudder to find Alec at the bedside, taking Simon's temperature.

'Sorry, I nodded off.'

'I don't wonder at it.' He held the slender tube to the light, shook down the mercury and replaced it in the glass. He looked at her with the air of a man who has been driven to a decision.

'I'm going to ring for the ambulance.'

'Alec! Is he—'

'Temperature's up a point.' His voice was calm but dull with conviction. 'It's no good, Grace. We can't supply adequate nursing here. You're all in – anyone would be. He'll have a better chance to pull through in hospital.'

Her tears came, helpless and painful. 'Now we'll have to tell Isobel.'

'No, not just yet. He is seriously ill, but we've still a little time before we decide.'

He went down to telephone. She pulled herself together, began to collect things Simon would need. When Alec came back he said: 'I'll go in the ambulance, of course. Now, about tonight. You're not fit to drive. And Martin can't take you – he must be on call. You'll have to get on to the local garage – Rogersons usually have a car available. Get them to drive you. Promise, now.'

She nodded. 'I promise.'

The ambulance arrived. Grace watched with an aching heart as the attendants carried Simon out on a stretcher, rolled in a red blanket. She watched the ambulance disappear down the village street; then there was just an empty bed, all the paraphernalia of the sick-room.

She sank down in a chair, buried her face in the bedclothes and cried. She had come here meaning to be everything to Simon, to give him all the care and attention she could possibly provide. Now a desolating sense of failure came. She should have known he would catch cold that day. She should have brought both boys to play in the garden, instead of leaving him by the ice-cold burn. Isobel, with her mother's sixth sense, would have done this. Now she felt she had let the sick woman down.

Exhausted and wretched, she was past reason, heaping blame on herself. Then she remembered to pray for Simon. A new strength and peace came to her. She splashed cold water on her face, then went downstairs.

Jess lingered in the hall, her eyes compassionate.

'Aye, it's hard to see the bairn go – but better for him, Miss Haydon. For he needs constant nursing, day and night, and that's something you canna manage.'

Grace nodded, not trusting herself to speak. 'Is Doctor Finch in?' she asked dully. She had an urge to speak to Martin, to hear the reassurances she hoped he would give.

Jess shook her head. 'He had an urgent call, just before the ambulance came. Went off in a right hurry.'

Grace nodded and lifted the telephone receiver. She called the local garage to ask about a car, listened in growing dismay to the apologies from Mr. Rogerson.

'It's away out, Miss Haydon – the two Miss Simms booked it for the whole day, off to see their brother in Edinburgh. No, it'll no' be back till after midnight.'

She thanked him and ended the call. Jess waited, her eyes enquiring. Grace explained what had happened.

'I'll just have to drive myself, that's all.'

'You're not fit!' Jess protested.

'I've got to.' Grace walked into the dining-room and poured herself a thimbleful of brandy. Her hands were trembling as she set down the glass. Her eyes felt full of hot sand and her knees were weak. She willed herself to find new strength. Isobel would be waiting for a visitor, and a visitor she should have.

It was a calm, sullen evening when Grace drove out on to the vale road. Long bars of dun-coloured cloud piled high towards the coast. She saw, as with a stranger's eyes, the new luxuriance of trees and roadside hedges. For her outdoor life had stopped some days ago.

At the crossroads she took the moor road down through Longframlington, which would later join the A.1. some miles short of the city. The traffic on this stretch was fairly light, the driving easy. She wound the window right down so that the fresh air would keep her alert. Subconsciously she identified each faint scent, the sweet musty smell from the sheep, the dew-drenched perfume of wild roses, the rank whiff of bracken. She breathed deeply, refreshing her tired lungs.

Within half an hour the stimulant of the brandy had worn off. Despite the breeze whipping her hair she found her brain clouding, her eyelids unbearably heavy. She realized with dismay that keeping awake required more than just an act of will. The very effort of concentration, of continually eyeing the road and her driving mirror, was in itself a dangerous soporific. Her senses swam. A terrible lassitude crept over her.

At the next lay-by she drew off the road, glanced at her watch. Perhaps if she dozed for ten minutes she might be able to slough off this dangerous urge to sleep, otherwise she would be a menace on the road.

She closed her eyes and sank low in the driving seat, conscious at first of the swish of passing traffic, the cry of peewits over the darkening moors, the sharp echoing bark of a dog from a nearby farm. Then even these faded. She lost consciousness.

The screech of tyres jarred her from sleep, followed by the slam of a car door, a voice at the window. She jerked into wakefulness, cruelly bewildered, wondering where she could be. Then the dashboard swam into view, the sight of another car parked just ahead.

'Are you ill?' the voice demanded.

She shivered, recognizing it, turned with sick apprehension to see Ellis Ridley's face framed in the window. His features were tense, his eyes alarmed.

'Grace, are you all right? I saw you with your head lolling, looking like nothing on earth. You haven't had an accident?'

'No, no.' She roused herself to sit upright, sent an agonized glance at her watch. Only seven minutes had passed.

'I just had to stop driving,' she explained. 'I was falling asleep.' She fumbled for the door handle. 'I'd better get out into the air.'

He helped her out. She had no wits to resist. Leaning against the car, she drew a couple of deep breaths. 'I'm all right now. I didn't know you were back.'

'I rang the surgery to ask after young Simon,' he said tersely. 'Jess told me the news. She said you were driving to Newcastle, though you were in no fit state to do it. I hoped I'd overtake you, and thank heaven I did. I'll take you the rest of the way in my car.'

She eyed him doubtfully. The moment was unreal. In the soft evening light the traffic flashed by, leaving them isolated, curiously alone. He watched her calmly, as if challenging her to argue.

'But why should you?' she asked.

His eyes glinted. A sarcastic curve came to his mouth. 'A family in trouble – a man I like and respect at his wits' end about his son, his wife lying helpless in hospital . . . and you ask why should I? Your opinion of me is even lower than I thought.'

Her face flamed. Alec – he was thinking of Alec. He was merely offering the help that no man, even an

Ellis Ridley, could withhold in a time of crisis. *She* didn't come into it at all.

'Thank you,' she said at last. 'But where can I leave Alec's car?'

'There's a garage half a mile down the road. Drive yourself there and I'll pick you up. Go easy now.'

At the garage Ellis Ridley arranged for Alec's car to be delivered in the morning. Grace joined him in his car, thankful that her ordeal was at an end, and yet wondering if the present situation was much of an improvement. She found herself hoping he would let her sleep, that they need not talk.

He drove with relaxed efficiency and in complete silence. At first she sat rigidly by his side, torn between anxiety over Simon and the almost unbearable tension of this man's presence. But soon her head dropped. She dozed heavily, conscious of noise and movement but never fully roused until the city outskirts were reached.

'Better pull yourself together – we're nearly there.'

His terse warning cut through the veils of sleep. She pulled herself upright, took a furtive peep in her handbag mirror, seeing a wan and heavy-eyed face reflected there.

Ellis Ridley gave his full attention to the hazards of the city traffic. She might not have existed. Only when he pulled into the hospital car park did he turn to look at her.

'Think you can go through with it?'

'I've got to.'

'You look pretty rough.' Mercilessly his eyes measured the ruin of her face. She felt like weeping.

'I know,' she faltered. 'If Isobel notices I shall just have to say I've got a cold.'

He turned his wrist to look at his watch. 'You're

a little early, judging by the visiting time on that board. Shall I ring the Cottage Hospital for news of Simon? If it's good you'll find it easier to keep a cheerful face.'

Her heart pounded in panic. 'And if – he's worse?'

He spoke evenly. 'If he's worse, then I can always see Isobel instead of you.'

'You? What could you say?'

'I have a reputation for walking where angels fear to tread. Also I can keep a poker face while telling the most outrageous untruths – a habit regrettably learned in my childhood.' She fancied she heard a bitter tinge in his voice.

She hesitated. 'There's a phone box in the Out-patients Hall. I'll come with you.'

Ellis Ridley was in the box about three minutes, the longest minutes in her life. She read a notice over and over again: 'Out-patients are requested to present Appointment Cards at the First Window. . . .' Her body felt hollow and insubstantial.

At last he swung open the door, his dark face expressionless. Grace spoke faintly. 'How is he?'

'I managed to speak to Alec. Simon's settled in well. He's in an oxygen tent and seems to be responding a little.'

'Oh, thank heaven!' She reeled a little, faint with relief. A firm hand supported her elbow.

'Take it easy, now. Alec's staying the night at the hospital. Now, shall we go over to the Chest Block?'

He escorted her to the foot of the stairs, saying he would wait in the corridor. She felt calmer now. The news, if not exactly good, was at least reassuring. Yet when she mounted the stairs she felt curiously alone. She admitted that there was a silent strength in Ellis Ridley, a strength which had supported her so far whether she liked it or not. She had neither asked for nor wanted his help, but now without it she realized her own weakness.

Isobel greeted her with a rueful smile. 'Hallo, Grace. No Alec, then? Not *another* emergency?'

'He had to go with a patient to the Cottage Hospital.' Grace blessed the fact that the bright top light had been switched off, leaving only a soft reading-lamp over the bed. She drew her chair into the shadow.

'Oh, bad luck! But I mustn't be greedy. I know his patients need him too. How is he, Grace? And how is my baby?'

Grace felt that a half truth was better than a lie. 'He went paddling in the burn and got a bit of a chill.' She tried to speak casually. 'We packed him off to bed right away. . . . You'll be thinking I'm making a poor job of mother-substitute.'

'Oh, nonsense! Boys will be boys. You can't anticipate everything—' She broke off. 'Grace, are you sure he's all right? It *is* just a chill? And who's with him now?'

'He's a bit better tonight.' Grace blessed the circumstances which made this statement the exact truth. 'Alec says so, anyway. And Jess is helping out.'

'Oh well, if Alec says so!' But Isobel added anxiously: 'You'll keep him warm indoors until he's fit again, won't you? I know Simon – any excuse to be out of bed.'

'Don't worry – he'll be well looked after.' At this point Grace was so stricken by a memory of the real circumstances – the hospital bed, the anxious hovering father, the oxygen tent, that she was almost overcome. She seized some books from her holdall and said hastily: 'Some more reading matter. I got that one on

Border Ballads you wanted. They had it on the library van.'

'Oh, thanks.' Isobel's attention was diverted as she flicked over the pages.

'How are you keeping?' Grace asked next.

Isobel smiled wryly. 'I hate all that "I'm proper poorly" stuff. But actually I've been a bit down these last few days, just worrying about anything and nothing. I keep wondering what would happen if Simon had an accident and needed me.' Tears shone in her eyes. 'I've been a bit weepy. But don't tell Alec, will you?'

'Of course not.' Grace felt that this was one worry she could be trusted to keep from her brother-in-law. 'What does your doctor say?'

'Oh, just that it's an occupational risk of T.B. patients. We're all up one day and down the next. At least it does me good to know I'm not the only one.' She smiled. 'Now I'm allowed up in the day-room for a short time at midday I realize there are other women in worse cases – some with *several* children to worry about.'

The half hour seemed to stretch to infinity. Racked by tension, fighting against a draining weariness, and in constant fear that she should weaken and give the game away, Grace nevertheless stayed the course. Even when the bell rang she must sit a moment, disguise her relief and longing to escape. When she rose and came unthinkingly near to the light, Isobel gasped.

'Grace, you don't look too well yourself!'

Wild inspiration came. She patted her jaw. 'Toothache. It's been keeping me awake nights. I'll have to take the plunge and go the the dentist's.'

'Oh, poor you!' Isobel was all concern. 'Then I

mustn't keep you. You must be all in, with Simon on your hands—' She suddenly brightened. 'I could always ring Simon from the ward telephone. That might cheer us both up.'

Grace felt her heart plunge in panic. Shock tingled through her veins. Her brain refused to deal with this last hurdle. She stood staring at Isobel, wildly searching for inspiration, but none came.

Then Isobel's face fell again. 'No, I'm forgetting. He'd have to get out of bed to answer it. I'll leave it for a day or two.'

Grace kissed her goodbye and escaped. In the corridor she paused to draw breath. For one dreadful moment the worst had almost happened.

She pulled herself together. Even now there could be no relaxing. There still remained the drive home with Ellis Ridley and all the complex emotions his presence aroused.

He waited at the stair foot, as she descended with a stream of other visitors. His eyes coolly questioned her.

'It's all right,' she said. 'I'm sure Isobel suspected nothing.'

'Good for you.' He spoke curtly. 'And now – home, and the sooner the better. You look all in.'

Again the searching gaze, missing nothing of the ravage of stress. She remembered again Angela's words – 'Her looks have quite gone' – and then was angry with herself for caring.

'I won't talk to you,' he said, once they were in the car. 'Just forget where you are and try to sleep.'

The city behind them, they drove mile after mile in silence over the dark moors. At first she did no more than doze, conscious through her drowsiness of his figure at her side, the movement of his arms, the gear-changing on the hills. He was a better driver than Douglas, with all of his verve but in perfect control. This she sensed almost subconsciously.

They reached a stretch of flat tableland, where the steady motion lulled her into sick, heavy slumber.

She dreamed she was driving with Douglas. He teased her by continually pushing up the speed. They rounded a corner where a ravine fell from the edge of the road. The car skidded, spun, teetered on the edge—

She woke violently, screaming Douglas's name, found herself clutching at Ellis, heard his down-to-earth curse and felt the shock of brakes jammed on with force. The car jarred to a standstill by the verge, Ellis's arm thrown protectively between her and the windscreen.

'What the devil!' he demanded. 'Lucky we didn't both shoot through the glass. And for your information, I'm *not* Douglas.'

He took his arm away and switched on the interior light. Shaking and breathless, Grace settled back in her seat.

'I'm sorry. It was a nightmare.'

That scarred, self-possessed face showed no sign of similar shock. 'I can imagine!' he said dryly.

Grace struggled against a tendency to burst into tears.

'Don't tell me that dreaming of Douglas is necessarily a nightmare,' he challenged.

'I dreamed he was driving me and the car skidded. We were falling.'

'Old buried fears taking over your subconscious, no doubt. Remembering the way Douglas used to drive you, I often wondered if you would come unscathed through your engagement.'

Grace rose in fury to Douglas's defence.

'He took risks, I know. But he would never have put me purposely in danger.'

'Did I suggest that?' He switched off the light again. 'If you're quite recovered—'

'Thank you, yes.'

Grace dozed no more. Within minutes they arrived at the Abbotshaws road end, and by the time she had fully recovered her composure the headlights had revealed the open white gates of Lintlaw House.

The house door opened and a flood of light scythed the darkness. As Grace got out she heard Martin's concerned voice.

'Is that you, Grace?'

She saw his figure outlined in the doorway. A rush of thankfulness came, a sensation of safety and normality. She ran to him, found him holding her hands. 'Thank heaven you're safe! And there's better news from the Cottage Hospital. Simon's taken a definite turn for the better. I've just been on the phone.'

'Oh, Martin!' She swayed a little, weak with relief. He caught her, held her close.

'Steady, Grace, you're all in. Come and sit down—'

He broke off as Ellis Ridley approached, halting in the shadows. Martin exclaimed: 'Ridley, you here?'

'He drove me, Martin.'

Ellis Ridley's voice rasped from the darkness. 'I see you're in good hands, Grace. And I'm glad to hear about Simon. As my presence is obviously an embarrassment, I'll say good night.'

There came the slam of the car door, the scattering of gravel under the wheels, then the roar of the exhaust.

Grace became aware that she was in the living-room, being helped to an armchair. Martin was asking if she would prefer tea or a drink. She stared at him dazedly, only now realizing what she had done.

Ellis Ridley had supported her through a time of heavy stress and anxiety. Without him she might never have reached the hospital to allay Isobel's suspicions. The family crisis which was happily now lifting might have been tragically complicated but for his intervention.

And she had not thanked him! It was to Martin she had showed her relief. It was Martin's hands she had grasped, Martin's comfort she had sought.

Her heart sank. She had been churlish and ungrateful. Whatever Ellis Ridley had done in the past, there could be no excuse for such treatment. She knew she must apologize to him as soon as was humanly possible.

The thought distressed her. She refused Martin's ministrations and went straight up to bed. She slept deeply and woke to find sunshine streaming between the curtains and Jess at her elbow with a tea-tray.

'Oh, am I late?' Grace blinked at her in dismay. Jess did not usually arrive until nine-thirty.

'You're no' to worry, Miss Haydon. I'm early, for I didn't expect you'd feel like coping with breakfast. Now there's no call to fret. Doctor Haydon's back and with good news. The bairn's well out of danger. He'll be back home in a day or two, the doctor says. They won't want you in the surgery this morning, and by the looks of the weather it'll be a small one, anyway. . . . Oh, aye, and Mr. Ridley's had the doctor's car sent back. The garage man delivered it just now. So you've nothing to do but drink your tea and take it easy.'

Grace smiled her thankfulness. 'We've been through

a bad time, Jess, but the worst is over.'

'Aye, that it is. I couldn't get here this morning for folks asking how the bairn was. And it was right kind of Mr. Ridley to look after you, Miss Haydon. He phoned earlier to ask how you were.'

Jess's eyes gleamed with challenge. Grace remembered the apology she owed him, and her heart skipped a beat. Perhaps a letter would do, was her next cowardly thought. Then at least she would not have to face that annihilating stare. And come to that, his former apology had been by letter. She could pay him in the same coin.

Jess turned away. 'He's off again this morning, said he'd be away a day or two and to tell you. . . . Well, I'd better get on. There'll be some breakfast when you feel like coming down.'

'I'm getting up, Jess, thank you.'

Ellis Ridley had been at pains to announce his second departure. This was obviously a hint to her to collect Douglas's things while he was gone, as he had earlier suggested. As she dressed she reflected that with Simon away she would never have a better opportunity. Perhaps by tomorrow Martin would be taking his round in that direction and could give her a lift.

Downstairs, Grace went straight to the surgery to find Alec. Their greeting was quiet but moving. When Grace had heard the details of the night, from the first harrowing moments of crisis to the first signs of Simon's improvement, she told Alec in turn of her visit to Isobel.

'You're a wonder, Grace. You mean she didn't guess at all?' His eyes were warm.

'It was a near thing,' she confessed. 'Especially when she suggested phoning.'

He shuddered. 'A near thing, as you say. . . . We mustn't forget to thank Ridley, either. It was most generous and far-seeing of him to offer his help. But on the whole I wouldn't have expected less of him. Despite all the gossip, he's a man I respect.'

Grace was silent. She might have to acknowledge Ellis Ridley's help, but she could not join in Alec's admiration.

After breakfast she joined Martin in the stable-yard, where he was polishing his car ready for his round. The sun was hot in the sheltered space, with the deep shadow of a sycamore sharply etched on the pale cobblestones.

He exclaimed in pleasure at sight of her, 'Grace, you look a different girl, positively blooming. You were half dead last night.' He frowned. 'And no wonder, exposed to that fellow Ridley's company for hours on end.'

'He offered to drive me. Just as well he did, actually—'

'It was bad luck I had to stay on call,' he fretted. 'I wanted to take you. I can imagine how you felt, incarcerated with him.'

She was startled by his tone. 'I got there – that was all that really mattered.'

'It puts you under an obligation to him, though.' Martin touched up his bonnet hub, his face almost sulky. 'If you ask me, the sooner he hares off on another of his mysterious expeditions, the better.'

'Why?'

His smile was rueful. 'Can't you guess? I'm already beginning to claim territorial rights.'

'After one evening out?'

'You seemed glad enough to see me last night.' He

had forgotten his polishing. His expression was glum yet expectant.

'I was. To see a friendly face – it meant so much. I'd been under rather a strain—'

She hesitated, confused. 'I don't know what you must have thought of me, throwing myself into your arms like that.'

'I'm not complaining!' he smiled.

He asked her about her hospital visit. Later she said: 'Oh, by the way, what was your urgent call last night?'

'Mrs. Bowden, the gardener's wife at the Grange. Severe pain and vomiting, but I traced it to a gorge on shellfish. She'd been to Seahouses for the day.'

'Lucky it was nothing worse.' She turned to go, but Martin caught her arm.

'Grace, I know things aren't back to normal yet, but you haven't forgotten that we're going out together one evening?'

'You know I'd like to,' she said. She sensed a change of emotional climate, as if Martin had spurred himself to a further effort of intimacy. Surely he couldn't be jealous of Ellis Ridley, she asked herself. The very idea was absurd.

'Then that's settled. 'Bye, Grace – see you at lunch.' He swung himself into the car and drove off on his rounds. Grace watched him go. He need have no fears, she reflected. Simon's illness had served to show him in a more serious light, as a man genuinely concerned for others. She felt for him now a warm affection, but guessed his own emotions went deeper. Was it really fair to encourage him?

The truth was, her sense of loss over Douglas seemed curiously sharpened lately. She found herself remembering passionate kisses with an insistent clarity, conscious again of forces within herself which had lain so long dormant. The familiar surroundings might be responsible, or even the heightened perceptions which came with any time of shock or stress such as Simon's illness. She could not pinpoint the reasons, but felt herself spun helplessly by events, one with Abbotshaws and its destinies.

By the following day reports on Simon were so good that Alec confidently expected to bring him home within a couple of days. He was now recovered enough for visits and that evening Alec planned to take Grace to the Cottage Hospital while Martin handled the surgery. Alec would continue by car to Newcastle to visit Isobel and Grace return home by bus.

During the afternoon Alec had calls to make in the upper reaches of Coquetdale. He approved of Grace's suggestion that she should come along as far as Peppercorn.

'Pity Ridley's away, though,' he added. 'I might have looked in to thank him personally for his help the other night.'

It was a lush June afternoon as they drove out of the vale and into the hills. No longer blinded by anxiety, Grace saw her beloved countryside with new eyes. The time of may and lilac was over, but wild roses and honeysuckle rioted in the hedges above carpets of buttercups and speedwells. White campion starred the woodland verges and as they gained higher ground they saw below them in the vale the beginnings of hay harvest, the men and the tractor-cutters like child's toys in the sloping fields. In the pastures the fat lambs flourished, their tails trimmed against fly-strike. With rearing problems almost over, the shepherds would have only a brief respite before the arduous jobs of shearing and dipping.

'I've three calls before Peppercorn,' Alec announced, 'one of them not so pleasant. Pringle's wife will have to be admitted to hospital, and I must break the news today. Her specimen test shows distinct signs of diabetes. A few weeks of treatment will be necessary before she can cope with the condition at home. Heaven knows how they'll manage without her. Besides Pringle and his three sons there's an old bedridden mother – and only a girl as daily help. We shall probably have to admit the old lady too. So often the shortage of hospital beds can be traced to cases like this, where instead of one admission we have two. And if I know Mrs. Pringle she'll fly off the handle at the mere mention of hospital.'

'Poor old Alec,' Grace said. 'Don't you wish you'd been a farmer instead?'

'Sometimes,' he admitted. 'When I see them in a sunlit hayfield. But there's always the other side of the coin, digging sheep out of the snow in a blizzard. No, on the whole no regrets. It's a good life.' He glanced sideways. 'Not a bad life for a doctor's wife, either.'

'Meaning?'

'Oh, nothing. Just that I've seen young Finch giving you some thoughtful looks lately. I'm surprised he hasn't made better progress by now. The lads these days have no initiative, that's the trouble.'

'Maybe he hasn't had much encouragement,' she said mildly.

'That sounds like a hint to change the subject,' he laughed. 'All the same I shall watch the situation with interest. And for my own sake I'd like to see him settle down in the practice.'

Grace said no more. At each of Alec's calls she left

the car and lounged against sun-warmed stone walls at the roadside, revelling in the warmth. This was rolling moorland country just under the foothills. In private estates across the river exotic splashes of crimson, purple and scarlet rhododendrons climbed the heights. The wooded summits above were the haunt of wild roe-deer, reminding her of Simon and his wild goats. A green woodpecker dipped and climbed with a mocking call above a group of firs.

Then the car was climbing again between bare slopes which later in the season would be sheeted with purple ling. Alec still chatted about his cases. Grace gave him scant attention, for they were approaching the Goatshiels track. The usual tension gripped her. Alec was bound for High Haugh and dropped her at the foot of the Peppercorn track.

'Pick you up in an hour, roughly,' he said.

Alone, the silence seemed oppressive. The heat of the sun was trapped and intensified in this basin of the hills. A pair of black-headed gulls spun high in the clear air, changing direction and disappearing in the direction of the coast. She mounted steadily up the stony path, watched by the white-faced Cheviot sheep grazing on the unfenced verge.

She came within sight of Peppercorn, suffered again that wincing stab of recognition. Would she ever see this house without emotion? It was so lonely, so self-sufficient, so lost and secret in its fold of the hills.

Billy Middlemass, the combined groom and houseman, was mending the stable gate. He stopped work to greet her, a fair quiet young man about Martin's age.

'Hallo, Billy!'

'Nice to see ye again, Miss Haydon. Mr. Ridley said ye might be up. Did ye want to gan in the house, for

I've the key here.'

'Yes, please. I'm collecting some things of Douglas's—'

'Aye, ye'll be wanting his things. It was a sad business, Miss Haydon. But time's a great healer.'

She nodded, thinking assent was simpler. He unhooked the key from the tack room, and after a few casual remarks she made her way into the enclosed house-yard.

Indoors the house was silent, almost oppressive. As she came through the hall the hush was broken by the sonorous tick of the grandfather clock. Sunlight barred the Turkey-carpeted stairs, flushing the faded crimson to a deep raspberry tone. Dust motes danced in the warm beams. She climbed to the upper corridor and Douglas's old room.

She pushed open the door in a blind panic, expecting a violent assault on her emotions, but it did not come.

Instead came a sensation of unreality. The room was unnaturally tidy, the books marshalled exactly on the shelves, the bed stripped and the curtains half drawn; a mere shell which had once housed a vivid personality.

Now it seemed no longer his. When she had rung the curtains back on their pole the sunshine dispelled the last of her fears. There was nothing in this atmosphere to upset her.

It was a different matter when she turned to a side table. Here were piled several framed photographs, along with a snapshot album. The photographs were school groups and cricket teams, showing Douglas as a boy. She was moved but not distressed. This was a Douglas she had not known. The album was another story. Here she saw her earlier blooming self, riding with Douglas, swimming with him at Bamburgh, raising champagne glasses at a local ball. She paused longest over a snapshot of herself mounted on Black Bess, Douglas holding the bridle. Her own laughing face was almost plump in its rounded happiness. Strange, too, how Bess had played such a big part in their love affair. Between herself and the gentle, gallant mare there had existed a very special fellowship. Just to see again those mild, intelligent eyes, the proud arching neck, was to remember an aching procession of carefree days, of thrilling canters on the moors and the quiet jog-trot home in the fading light. Now Bess belonged to another owner, and Douglas – Douglas—

Sharply she closed the book. Here in this house she felt too vulnerable for further pain. The rest must wait until she was home.

She examined the books, from childhood favourites through tales of war and adventure, to textbooks on estate management and auction practice. His whole short, racy life was here.

She was leafing through a Nevil Shute when a slip of paper fluttered to the floor. Retrieving it, she found a list of cattle prices jotted on the back of a sheet of handwriting. Reversing it, she found the last paragraph of a letter, together with a signature.

– 'I know better than to come to the house, though,' she read. 'I'll wait at the usual place. Please come, Douglas darling. You wouldn't like me to get impatient and do something we'd both be sorry for, would you? But you know the last thing I want to do is hurt you. Yours always, Wyn.'

She eyed the words uneasily. Before meeting her Douglas had dated many girls, but she had never heard him mention a Wyn, unless this was a nickname.

The hidden threat chilled her, the mystery nagged at her mind. At last she shrugged and returned the sheet to the book. She would never know, anyway. It was silly to worry. And whoever Wyn was, her power to hurt had gone.

Now, though, she had no heart to stay longer. She stacked together a few selected books, the photographs and the album, and stowed them in a canvas holdall from the wardrobe. She drew the curtains, took a last look at the blank shadowed room and went downstairs.

In the hall she produced a square envelope from her handbag, the letter of apology to Ellis Ridley. She propped it against the telephone and took a last look round. This was most certainly the last time she would ever be here.

Her eyes misted. She moved blindly towards the door leading to the back premises. Then she hesitated. The nostalgia was hers alone. The house itself, she felt, throbbed not with past but with present life, as though its owner had imparted to it some of his own intense magnetism. She found within herself a strange reaction, almost a quickening of response. A moment later she violently rejected it.

'Good-bye, Peppercorn,' she whispered.

CHAPTER SIX

WHEN Grace walked into the stableyard she saw a scene of activity at the gate. A man was just lifting the ramp of an empty horsebox, assisted by Billy Middlemass. She heard a whicker from the stable and guessed at a new arrival. In the old days there had never been less than four horses about the place, Douglas and Ellis with at least one hunter each and sometimes a colt to be schooled for a friend, or a mare on trial.

The whicker became a loud whinny. She stopped, her heart jerking in disbelief. The sunlight was trapped, hot and sleepy, in the cobbled enclosure. A Labrador watchdog panted in the shade. She could hear Billy Middlemass shouting a farewell to the man with the horsebox. She stared, blinked and stared again. A big winsome mare, coal-black except for a white star on her forehead, ears pricked forward, was watching her with still liquid eyes. Then again came that excited whinny of recognition, a hollow stamping of hooves behind the half-door.

She cried out: 'Black Bess! ... Oh, Bess, it *is* you! You've come back!'

She allowed the mare to muzzle softly over her face. She laid her head against the great sinewy neck. 'Bess, you knew me, you knew me!'

And now at last her tears spilled, the yard rocked in a haze. She wept a little in her happiness.

A voice roused her. She blinked away her tears and saw Angela before her, trim and composed in riding clothes, a treacherous smile on her face.

'Well, well, how touching! When the glad reunion's over I'd like to ride my mare.'

Grace mopped her eyes, angry and ashamed to be found so. She drew her hand from the mare's neck. Bess turned bright eyes towards her, softly watchful.

'Your – mare?'

Angela smiled. 'Yes. Any objection? Ellis bought her back – for me.'

The heat seemed suddenly unsupportable. Grace felt stifled, bewildered. 'Why Bess?' she asked. 'You've never seen her before. You were away when—' She broke off. 'I suppose she was going cheap?'

Angela shrugged. 'You know Ellis – he always drives a hard bargain where horseflesh is concerned.'

Horseflesh. For one incredulous moment Grace had supposed Ellis had relented, had bought back Bess for sentimental reasons. Angela's cold words banished this ridiculous fancy.

She picked up her holdall, said shakily: 'I must go. I've just been collecting some of Douglas's things.'

'Really?' Angela reached into the tack-room for a gleaming bridle. 'I imagine Ellis will be relieved. And I've certainly no taste for a house full of sentimental relics.'

Grace spoke at white heat. 'Ellis may think he can drive out the memory of Douglas – you too for that matter. But he'll always be here – for me!'

Angela watched her in hard amusement. 'Poor little Grace – still clinging to your illusions?'

'I don't know what you mean.'

Billy Middlemass approached. 'Ye'll no' be thinking of riding her yet, Miss Forster? I'd give her time to settle down first. She'll be on the fresh side, I'm fearing.'

'Oh, nonsense.' Angela caught at the mare's head collar. 'I hope I can handle anything Miss Haydon has ridden.'

Grace saw Bess's ears flatten, saw apprehension in the dark liquid eyes, heard hooves backing in panic on the brick floor. Bess needed gentle but firm handling, and Angela, she knew, had a cruel hand with a horse. She turned to go, a helpless ache in her heart, but caught a beaming smile from Billy.

'I clean forgot to tell you Bess was coming back today, Miss Haydon. Did she know you?'

She nodded. 'It's lovely to see her again.' Tears rushed to her eyes and she turned away quickly. 'Good-bye, Billy.'

She trudged down the hill track with her heavy bag. This was the end, the very end now. She would never see Peppercorn again, and had not even the heart to turn for a last look. Black Bess was home, but Angela would be her mistress, and all that remained of the old life was this bag full of relics.

This afternoon's work might have held a healing touch, like the cauterizing of a wound, but for the last cruel twist of Bess's return. She knew now that Ellis Ridley was a man entirely without finer feelings. To sell Bess had been bad enough; to acquire her again simply as a business proposition, to give her to Angela when he knew the pain such ownership would cause *her* – it was contemptible.

She sat at the footpath waiting for Alec, watching a couple of greyling butterflies flit over the still bracken. Almost she regretted leaving that note of apology. And yet wasn't Angela the real cause of her resentment; Angela at home in the stables, in possession of Bess, acting already as the new bride of Peppercorn. She saw now, quite clearly, that relinquishing the old rights was a pain she could have overcome. Relinquishing them to Angela – that was the rub. This twisting pain in her heart was plain simple jealousy.

But why? It was laughable to think *she* should want Ellis Ridley for a husband. She could only put it down to that fatal resemblance between the two men. Her reaction was purely automatic and subconscious.

Then why nurse an aching heart, when she could reason away the cause? Yet her heart continued to ache, deaf and blind to reason.

Going home in the car with Alec she remembered again Angela's words: 'Still clinging to your illusions?' What had she meant? She wondered again uneasily about the scrap of letter, the name 'Wyn'.

Cautiously she sounded Alec on the subject. He shook his head.

'No, can't say I've met anyone called Wyn. What's it all about?'

'Oh, just a name among Douglas's things. I wondered if she was an old flame.' She spoke lightly.

'Well, it's no secret to you that he had plenty. But that was before your time, so why worry?'

'Just curiosity,' she smiled. But she fancied he gave her a concerned look.

That evening she visited Simon, as planned. He was quite weak, but rational, his rusty mop of hair fiery against his washed-out cheeks. She was deeply thankful to find him quite cheerful and self-possessed. Hospitals and their equipment and routine held no fears for a doctor's child. In fact he was so eager to explain everything to her she had to chide him for talking too much.

'Save it for when you get home,' she coaxed.

'How are Nelson and Napoleon?' he demanded next. 'You didn't forget to feed them, did you?'

'Of course not.'

'And their water?'

'And their water, gallons of it.'

'Have you been to see old Will?'

'No. We've all been far too busy. I'll take you when you're better.'

Simon nodded in satisfaction. 'I'll tell him all about going in the ambulance. I bet he's never been. Oh, gosh, here's Nurse with my hot milk. She makes me drink every drop.' He pulled a face.

'Good for her!' Grace bent to kiss him good-bye. 'You just do everything you're told, and then you'll be home all the sooner.'

It was actually two days later when he was discharged, with a further week's bed rest ahead. Isobel knew he was still laid up and had been thus easily dissuaded against her plan of telephoning. Instead Alec had proposed bringing Simon to the hospital as soon as possible, so that she could see him from the ward window. The plan won her instant approval.

At home Simon too approved. 'Yes, I'd like that,' he said calmly. 'It might do Mummy a bit of good. She must be fretting for me.'

Alec and Grace saved their rueful laughter until they were downstairs. 'Isn't it just like the thing,' Alec mused. 'There we were leaning over backwards to arrange it for his sake, and now he's graciously agreeing to it for his mother's. Just like a child! The illness has washed his fretting clean out of his mind. Though I must say the cure was worse than the disease.' He added: 'All the same, Isobel will want to telephone eventually. I shall have to warn Simon not to mention his stay in hospital.'

The week of Simon's bed-rest was dull and cool, though most of the vale's first crop of hay was baled and stored before rain and mist blotted out the hills. In such weather Simon was content to play propped up in bed. Later in the week he was allowed up for an hour to watch children's programmes on television. By the week-end the heavy skies had broken, with promise of further fine weather, and Simon was up all day.

Gradually Grace resumed her surgery work and Lintlaw House slid back into its normal routine. Jess had worked overtime on the domestic side and Grace begged her to take a few days off once Simon was able to return to school. Jess refused.

'A bit of extra work never hurt a body, and the doctor paid me well for my trouble. . . . Eh, it's grand to have the bit laddie nearly well again. My old dad's asked for him every day. You'll be bringing the bairn in to see him soon, Miss Haydon?'

Grace promised to do so. She had been greatly touched by the general concern for Simon. In Abbotshaws joys and troubles were for sharing. Even the ubiquitous Archie Scott had called with the present of a lethal-looking pea-shooter, which Alec had begged Grace to 'lose' as soon as possible.

She was touched, too, by Martin's attitude to Simon. He exerted himself daily to amuse the convalescent child, one day bringing in a giant jig-saw, the next a Chinese puzzle or just a demonstration of a new knot. The old teasing banter returned, the memorizing of Scout lore and the solemn discussions on birds and animals.

'He's learning, Auntie Grace. He can tell a pigeon

from a peewit now.'

'Would you call that progress?' Martin asked in mock anxiety.

Alec raised an eyebrow. 'We won't give him a medal yet. He still calls rams ewes and a fine field of oats is still hay. He goes to treat farmers for rheumatism and ends by giving them apoplexy.'

Martin laughed in good humour, but winked at Grace. She seemed to detect in him lately a conscious effort to identify himself with family life. And she wondered if it could be for her sake.

After a few days on his feet Simon duly went with Alec to the Newcastle hospital and mother and son had the comfort of glimpsing each other, if only through glass. Isobel's window was mercifully on the third floor. Had she been nearer she would most certainly have seen that Simon was far from his usual robust self.

At home again, when Simon was in bed, Alec said: 'That's the last hedge taken now, I hope. I feel I can stop worrying. Of course I shall tell Isobel the whole truth once she's home again.'

Grace drew the curtains against the fading dusk. 'Any news about that?'

'Not exactly. But Sutcliff, the consultant, says she may be able to come home for a week-end before long. The danger of infection will be gone by that time. And this is the general thing now, a process of gradual rehabilitation.'

'Does Isobel know?'

'Not yet. He doesn't want to build her hopes and perhaps find she has a setback. Best to live through one day at a time.'

She sat down by the fire. 'It's been a hard row to

hoe, Alec,' she said gently, using an old country saying. 'You've held up wonderfully.'

He knocked out his pipe. 'Case of having to. At least the patients haven't been neglected. It's a great relief to have an able partner. And Martin hasn't grumbled at the extra work.'

Grace reflected that this might be so, but that it was Alec's quiet strength which had been their mainstay. If he had cracked it would have been complete disaster. She had often teased and criticized her brother for a certain rigidity, a lack of imagination; but now she could see that these very traits had proved valuable assets in their emergency.

He stood up and fitted his pipe in the rack. 'We couldn't have weathered it without you, Gay. I was just talking to Ridley yesterday—'

Grace stiffened. She bent to tidy the magazine rack, her face hidden. 'Is he home again, then?'

'What? . . . Oh yes. I'd a call to make at Burnhead. Old Mrs. Wylie fell and sprained her wrist. I met him just past Burnhead Pike, exercising a horse, and he stopped me to ask after Simon. He was praising you, too. Said it took guts to take a car out the way you were that night. He seemed most impressed.'

The blood rode up her face. 'Condescending of him!'

'He didn't mean it that way.' Alec's voice sharpened. 'Give the man credit for a genuine compliment, Grace.'

She felt roused enough to argue, but Alec had turned to wind the clock. They were both tired and more than ready for bed. And it was, in any case, an argument which could have no satisfactory conclusion.

Three days later Grace took Simon on the promised visit to old Will. Jess received them gladly and they found little change in the cottage scene. White roses now bowered the doorway, but there was still a low fire in the grate. 'I just like to know it's there,' she explained. 'The weather can be that changeable. And if Dad's feeling the chill I can just throw on a faggot of wood and get a nice blaze.'

Old Will sat propped up in bed as always, with Moss lying on the plaid rug. The plumy tail beat feebly at their entrance, the old eyes brightened. Will laid aside his pegging to greet them, his face furrowed in a deep smile.

'Well, ma laddie, so you're on your feet again! You're luckier nor me! And away in yon grand ambulance! Man, but ye'll be ower proud to talk to your auld friends. Come away in, Miss Haydon. Ye'll have had a busy time nursing him, forbye.'

Simon chatted happily to the old man, stroked Moss and boasted about his stay in hospital. He ended by inspecting the latest rug, an arresting affair of green and violet. He spelled out: 'Rest – in – the—'

'Rest in the Lord, ma laddie. It's a short easy one, d'ye see. I'm getting rare and lazy in my old age.'

Jess was busy showing Grace a tablecloth she was embroidering for the church sale, then begged advice on the cutting out of a dress. Grace reflected that Simon's illness had removed much of the older woman's reserve. They were easier with each other and she was glad of it.

She became aware of Simon's excited voice.

'But did you ever see any wild goats at Goatshiels? Mr. Ridley said they used to be there.'

'Ah, that would be at the High Stones. Aye, they

were there right enough, years ago, forbye the herd at Thrunton Crags.'

'Will they ever come back to Goatshiels, Mr. Robson?'

'They might, laddie.'

'But how would they come back?' the child insisted. 'Where would they come from?'

'Well now, it could be this way. There'd be an old male goat, maybe, astray from another herd, over the back o' the Cheviots. He could meet up with a nanny who'd lost her way, or maybe be a tame goat who'd got loose. Then they'd mate and begin breeding, start their own herd—'

'Now, now, Father, you'll be filling the laddie's head with rubbish,' Jess broke in. 'He's got daft fancies enough.'

Old Will peered from under busy white eyebrows at Grace.

'Aye, and I was forgetting mysel'. I'd no right to talk of Goatshiels in front of Miss Haydon. I beg pardon, miss, for it slipped out without thinking.'

'It doesn't matter, Mr. Robson,' Grace said quietly, as Jess set out the tea-cups. 'I don't expect people to worry about my feelings. In fact I'd much rather they didn't.'

'Aye, they're wise words ... Ye were fond o' the High Stones, though, Miss Haydon?'

'The High Stones?' she faltered.

'I was shepherd over at Goatshiels Hope that year, at Ned Grahamslaw's. He was my last master before I took ill. And many's the time I spied ye up there with Mr. Douglas.'

'You – saw me?' Grace's heart began to race. 'But—'

'Aye. I was a good way off, up near Drylaw, but I've aye had good eyes. There was no mistaking your bonnie hair, for it showed up bright against the rocks. Time and again I saw ye. But there, I'm distressing you, Miss Haydon.'

She forced herself to pursue the point. 'Just a minute, Mr. Robson, I want to get this right. You're talking about two summers ago?'

'I'm bound to be, lassie, for I was laid up by the next winter, and haven't set foot outside the garden since.'

'And you saw me – several times?'

'Times out o' number, towards evening time, when the sun was just going.'

Grace hesitated. Jess stood arrested in the kitchen doorway, a milk jug in her hand, her face a mixture of interest and apprehension.

Grace made a determined effort at control, though her heavy heartbeats were almost suffocating. She forced a smile.

'Your eyesight *must* be good,' she said at last.

Jess visibly relaxed, and hustled to the table. Simon, who had been fondling Moss, turned to ask the old man a question, and the moment passed.

Grace studied the dress pattern again, her thoughts melting in confusion.

Douglas at the High Stones, times out of number, meeting a girl with red hair?

Not herself. Impossible. She had been only once to the High Stones with Douglas. It was a difficult, isolated climb. It couldn't have been Douglas, then. Old Will's eyesight could have deceived him. And yet there was that look of arrested alarm in Jess's face.

Other thoughts rushed in a torrent, overwhelming her.

Angela's voice: 'Still clinging to your illusions?'

The letter, signed 'Wyn': 'I will meet you at the usual place.'

That time Douglas had arrived late, full of excuses . . .

And again Jess's hints that Ellis did not approve of his brother's 'goings-on'.

What was this? A monstrous plot to damage her memory of Douglas? Or was she exaggerating the importance of slight incidents, chance remarks, none of which could hold meaning if old Will had mistaken another man for Douglas?

Then her heart almost stopped. Douglas had died at the High Stones. What was he doing there that evening? She had always previously imagined some innocent purpose. The path, though perilous, was a short cut to a lone farm in the next valley. Now a much more sinister reason appeared.

'Are you feeling all right, Miss Haydon?' Jess asked, the teapot poised in her hand.

Grace roused herself. 'Of course, Jess, but I'll just move back from the fire. I'm feeling the heat.'

She detected in Jess's eyes a look of genuine pity. Her heart sank again. As soon as the ritual cup of tea and buttered scone had been taken she made an excuse to leave.

All the way home Simon chattered. Several times the words 'wild goats' impinged on her consciousness, but otherwise his talk was gibberish. Her brain was still grappling with the mystery of the High Stones.

That evening surgery was busy. Grace worked without stopping at the business of finding records, attending dressings and chaperoning where necessary, besides dealing with callers for medicine. It was Martin's turn on duty. The local dialect no longer confused him and he was beginning to reflect some of Alec's patience with the halting description of symptoms.

'More of a burning pain, Doctor. I noticed it when I was churning, but thought nowt about it. The times I've been on to my man for a new one, but we'd had a bad year—'

'Yes, but what about the pain, Mrs. Turnbull?'

'That's just what I'm saying, Doctor. It was the churning—'

When Mrs. Turnbull had gone, clutching her prescription, Martin grinned.

'I'm getting the rhythm of it, you must admit. Let them run on obbligato for so long, then pounce!'

She laughed. 'It's Mrs. Willson next, with the twins. You remember they had mumps?'

Martin glanced at the clock and groaned. 'How many more after Mrs. Willson?'

'Five – no, six.'

'Stone the crows! We'll be here for an hour yet. And do I hear another car drawing up?' But his rueful smile was good-natured enough.

Eventually the last patient left, the records were put away, and the dispensary cleared. Grace had left Simon playing with his fort in the living-room. His bedtime was the next thing. Still in her white overall, she crossed the hall.

She hesitated, hearing voices from inside the room. Through the open front door she saw Ellis Ridley's car in the drive. Her face burned. When she went in Ellis was sprawled on the rug with Simon, playing soldiers.

He looked up, gave her a brief smile and got to his feet without haste. 'Good evening, Grace. Surgery over?'

'Yes.' She met his eyes. 'Alec isn't back from Newcastle yet. Did you want him?'

Simon nudged her. 'Auntie Grace, look what I've got! Mr. Ridley brought me some more soldiers for my fort. Scottish ones with kilts. Aren't they super?'

His delight was touching. She smiled down at him. 'They're very fine, aren't they? Did you say thank you?'

' 'Course I did! Mr. Ridley got these ones in Newcastle.'

Grace said stiffly: 'Very kind of you.' She turned to Simon. 'It's long past your bedtime. You run upstairs now, and I'll come when I've heated your milk.'

He pouted. 'But I've only just started to play with these new ones. They're foot soldiers, you know. And they've got their own flag, but Mr. Ridley says it's always called "The Colours".'

Ellis said crisply: 'A good soldier obeys commands at the double. Right – attention! Pack kit and quick march to the stairs!'

After a startled, respectful look, Simon jerked into action.

'I'm all ready, Mr. Ridley.' He stood holding his fort. 'Will you listen to me marching upstairs?'

'I'll be listening. I want a smart turn at the top and a halt-left-right-left-right at your bedroom door. Then you'll hear me give the "dismiss". Right?'

'Right, Mr. Ridley.'

Ellis followed him into the hall. The impressive

little ceremony over, he almost cannoned into Grace trying to escape to the kitchen. He held her arm with an easy authority. 'Where are you going?'

'Simon's milk – the kitchen—' she stammered.

'In a moment.' He steered her firmly into the room and shut the door. 'How are you feeling now?'

'How am I – Oh, you mean after that night? No ill-effects.' She crimsoned under his hard gaze. 'I went to Peppercorn for the things. I left a note.'

'Thank you, I got it.' His stare pinned her down. 'I appreciated the apology.' He added on a lighter note: 'You collected everything you wanted?'

'Yes, thank you.'

His tall form barred the way to the door. She felt trapped and breathless. He was formally dressed this time, the dark suit and sober tie somehow highlighting that shining furrowed scar on his temple.

'Did you see Black Bess?' he asked.

'Yes.' Her tone quickened and deepened. 'Angela told me you'd bought her back – at another bargain price, I suppose?'

He shook his head. His stormy grey eyes were intimidating, and she ached to escape. 'No, no bargains this time. Her owner took full advantage of the fact that I wanted her back. In fact I paid through the nose for her.'

'I hope Angela was grateful.'

'Angela?' He frowned.

'Angela told me Black Bess was for her.'

He smiled a little. 'Angela is subject to flights of fancy. Black Bess was not for her. She has mounts of her own. She offered to exercise Bess for me – not quite the same thing, you'll agree.'

'Then why?' she asked blankly.

He offered her a cigarette, but she shook her head. Lighting one himself, he strolled to the window. Her way of escape was now open, but her feet seemed rooted to the floor.

'No,' he repeated, 'Bess was not for Angela.' He swung to face her. 'I bought Black Bess for you!'

'For – me?'

'Yes. You remember that day at Peppercorn when I said you ought to ride again. I realized then just how much Bess had meant to you, and that perhaps I was wrong in not consulting your wishes before selling her. Though at the time my reasons seemed logical. You had gone away and my weight is too heavy for Bess – you may remember Douglas was a good deal lighter?'

She remained silent, her heart racing. He went on:

'When I began the transaction I had every hope you might accept her as a gift. That was before I fully discovered how much you loathed and resented me.' He shrugged. 'An error of judgment on my part. Am I right in supposing the gift would be refused?'

She could find no immediate words, still struggling between amazement and guilt. She too, had made an error of judgment, had classed him as a heartless monster. And Bess . . . If circumstances had been different, Bess might have been hers.

'I asked you a question, Grace.'

'You know the answer already—' she began, when Martin came into the room. His candid blue eyes scanned both their faces. 'Hallo, Ridley. Am I intruding?'

'No, of course not,' Grace said. 'Excuse me, I must see to Simon.'

She hurried out to the kitchen, began warming milk. Her brain whirled. She could scarcely grasp even now the magnitude of Ellis Ridley's offer. Could this be in the nature of an atonement, or an assuaging of his own guilt?

She took the milk upstairs, tucked Simon up and kissed him good-night. Then she stripped off her white overall and tidied her hair.

She longed to stay in the seclusion of her room until Ellis had gone, but this could not be. He deserved the courtesy of thanks and a parting word.

As she reached the hall he came suddenly from the living-room. Seeing her, he closed the door smartly behind him.

'Thank you for calling,' she faltered. 'I – appreciate your thought about Black Bess. But I'm afraid there can be no question—'

'Think no more of it!' His words lashed her. 'It was presumptuous of me. And if I've embarrassed you I apologize.' He smiled grimly. 'I believe Doctor Finch is waiting in there for you, and I imagine from his attitude he suspects my attentions.' He turned away with a mocking glance. 'But you and I, Grace – we know just how little he need worry, don't we? Good-night!'

She remained frozen until his car left the drive. Then she went slowly into the living-room. Martin was at the window watching Ellis's departure. He swung to face her, his eyes troubled.

'Grace, will you tell me something, honestly?'

'Yes, if I can.'

'Just how serious is Ellis Ridley about you?' he demanded.

'Ellis Ridley – serious about me?' Her face

flamed. 'Martin, that's absurd, and you know it.'

She sank down on the nearest chair, shocked and trembling.

Martin's gaze was uncertain. 'I'm judging by appearances, Grace. He always seems to be dancing attendance these days.'

'Ellis Ridley – dancing attendance – on me? Oh, Martin, surely not. And anyway, what about Angela?'

'I know all about Angela. I just – can't make up my mind.' He coloured. 'A man likes to know where he stands, that's all.' He added, almost as an afterthought: 'And you did promise me another date.'

'I know I did.' She was calmer now. 'And I meant it.' She told herself it was ridiculous to be so disturbed. Martin had assumed mistaken motives for Ellis Ridley's actions, that was all.

Martin pressed; 'You don't think Ridley means anything, then?'

'How could he? He knows my opinion of him too well.' She was amazed at his insistence.

'That could be enough of a challenge for a man like him.'

She shook her head. 'No, Martin, you're mistaken. The whole idea's ridiculous.'

'You're certain he means to have Angela, then?'

'It's not just my opinion. Everyone thinks so, Angela included.'

'Then I suppose you're right ... When will you come out with me again, Grace? I'm free tomorrow evening. I suppose Peggy would baby-sit?'

'I'm sure she would.' Grace brightened. 'Tomorrow, then. I must say I feel like a break, after all the worry over Simon.'

'Where would you like to go? The bright lights, or

a country inn?'

'Shall we wait and see what mood strikes us?' she smiled. Martin seemed still preoccupied, almost uneasy. His obvious jealousy had startled her. It seemed out of character. He looked absurdly boyish standing there, one hand fiddling with a paperweight on the bureau.

She jumped up. 'I must see to supper.'

'Grace!' His tone was pleading. He walked towards her, caught her hand. 'Tomorrow I may have something to say to you. I mean it won't be just an ordinary date. I don't quite know how to say this, but I thought you deserved fair warning.'

A rush of confused thoughts came. She hadn't expected a proposal yet. She pressed his hand lightly, then removed her own. 'Thanks, Martin – for the warning, I mean. Excuse me now, won't you?'

He smiled into her eyes, his own wistful. 'Tomorrow, then, about seven?'

She nodded and left the room.

The following evening there was no surgery. Alec was not visiting Isobel but remained on call. Peggy Everitt arrived just after Simon's bedtime and Grace lingered to chat while Martin made an adjustment to his car.

'My sister's home on holiday,' Peggy volunteered, as she unrolled some bright blue knitting. 'I'm doing this sweater for her. Freda's got three weeks off – I think I told you she's a nurse, in a Manchester hospital now. She makes me right envious. But I've always been a home bird. I like to see Mam every day.'

'I don't blame you. You're young enough yet to go out into the world. I suppose your sister finds Abbotshaws rather quiet now?'

'Aye, she does. She's changed a lot, our Freda. There, I shouldn't have called her that. She doesn't like it now.'

'What name does she like?' Grace hunted along the mantelpiece for her lighter.

'Her name's Winifred, really . . . Is there anything wrong, Miss Haydon?'

Grace found herself staring. 'No, no. What were you going to say, Peggy?'

'She likes to be called Wyn now, but Mam doesn't like it.'

Grace said faintly: 'She's the one with the red hair, isn't she?'

'Aye, that's right,' Peggy rattled on. 'Takes after Dad, though he's more plain ginger. Mind, Wyn's quieter in some ways. She's no' nearly as wild as she was. All the lads in the district were after her.'

Grace pretended to adjust the T.V. ready for Peggy. Her senses swam. She said lightly: 'Didn't your sister go out with Mr. Ridley at one time – Douglas, I mean?'

'Aye, she did. But that was before you were engaged to him, Miss Haydon. He was keen enough for a time – And *she* liked him. But she always had plenty others lined up. Then by the time you came here to work she was living over at Rothbury, chambermaid in a hotel. That's how you've never run across her, I expect.'

'I expect so.' Grace stood a moment, irresolute. 'I'm going now, Peggy. I don't think Simon will wake up, and Doctor Haydon will let you know if he has to go out. I hope you'll be comfortable.'

'I'll be fine. Just you away out and enjoy yourself, now.'

'Enjoy' was perhaps an unfortunate word. Grace did not join Martin immediately, but slipped into the small cloakroom off the hall and bolted the door. She leaned her back to it, her thoughts spilling in confusion.

So Wyn was Peggy's sister. So much she knew now. According to Peggy, Wyn's affair with Douglas had ended with her departure to Rothbury. And so, as far as any local knowledge was concerned, it might well have done. But Rothbury was no further from Peppercorn than was Abbotshaws, only on the opposite side. And old Will had seen Douglas, 'times out of number', with a red-haired girl at the High Stones. And this during his engagement. The chill of absolute conviction came. Douglas had been deceiving her all along.

She was stricken, helplessly angry, deeply humiliated. Her face burned. So Jess had been right to speak of his goings-on. There was nothing, after all, to choose between the two brothers. Both were treacherous, both weak where women were concerned. Of the two, she told herself she now preferred Ellis. At least he made no secret of his failings.

Such was her immediate reaction, bitter and violent.

Memories clawed her, of soft spoken words she now knew to be lies, of kisses of betrayal, of tears she need never have wept. She had no doubt, even now, that Douglas would have honoured his marriage proposal, would have carried his deceit and double-dealing to the very altar and even beyond. Wyn was not the kind of girl he would ever marry. He just wanted to have his cake and eat it too.

How many people had known, was her next wounding question. Possibly Jess, most certainly Ellis

. . . Her humiliation deepened.

She roused herself at last. Martin was waiting. Martin, who clearly loved her and wanted her. She would go to him, she would listen to his proposal.

She might even say yes.

CHAPTER SEVEN

MARTIN had brought his car to the door. As Grace approached him he said anxiously: 'Anything wrong?'

She shook her head.

'But you look—' He broke off. 'You've come to say you'd rather not go out, is that it?'

'No, of course not. It's just – something I heard. Let's forget it.'

'If that's how you want it. But answer me one thing first. Was it something about me?'

'No!' She smiled. 'Why, have you any dark guilty secrets?'

'Not so you'd notice. . . . Well, where shall we go?'

In the end they settled to dine at an old inn near Wooler and sat afterwards over coffee and drinks in an almost deserted lounge.

Grace was making a valiant effort to appear normal. Resolutely she dismissed Douglas's treachery from her mind, discussed subjects from medicine to films. Then came a silence. Martin gave her a queer dubious smile and reached for her hand.

'Well, Grace, this is it. You must know what I'm going to ask you.'

Far away in the depths of the hotel a telephone rang. It woke an echo of alarm in her heart. But she said calmly: 'What is it, Martin?'

He looked curiously resigned. 'I just want to know – is there any chance you'll ever forget Douglas and marry me?'

She smiled. 'Do you think it would work?' She was playing for time, a little uneasy.

'I'm sure it would. We're right for each other, if that means anything.'

For a proposal, she felt it was surprisingly flat. She sat twirling the stem of her glass. 'Not always. Two people can seem so right for each other – but are they? And two others – you hear everyone say, "What on earth did they see in each other?" But if there's a violent attraction, incompatibility doesn't seem important.'

'You really think that?' His sudden eagerness startled her. She could not quite understand him.

'It was like that with Douglas – at first—' Her voice faltered.

'You mean he wasn't really good enough for you? But even that couldn't change your feeling for him?'

She was silent. In a way he was right. She had forgiven all his faults. Only this last one, unfaithfulness, she could not have borne. . . .

She collected her thoughts. What was wrong with Martin? Surely he wasn't suggesting he was violently attracted to her? The very tone of his proposal belied that. She heard him say:

'I've made a mess of this, Grace. You must have guessed the real truth by this time.'

He was embarrassed, almost beseeching. 'You know, don't you, that I'm asking you on the rebound?'

'Martin! Are you serious?'

'Yes. Never more so.'

'You mean – Angela?'

He nodded, colouring. His strange vacillation was explained. She began to grasp the truth. 'You mean that last night, when you asked if Ellis was serious about me, it was because you wanted to know if Angela—'

'Exactly. Oh, I've been a clumsy blundering fool. Though I did try to wrap it up as best I could. Grace, look – I think the world of you. I know in my heart you're worth ten of Angela. . . . But I *love* her.' His eyes were despairing. 'When I'm near her I can't see or hear properly. She just needs to crook her little finger to get me jumping through hoops. . . . And the worst of it is, I don't even like her as a person. It's all purely chemical.'

His desperate honesty touched her, but his words had a much stronger effect. It was as though he struck a thunderous echo in her own heart. Martin might have been describing her own reactions to Ellis's nearness. 'I can't see or hear properly . . . I don't even like her—'

Yes, she too knew these violent emotions. She was swayed by tremendous forces. This was what drew Ellis and herself into continuing conflict. All along she had been blaming Ellis's resemblance to Douglas. Only now, with her illusions completely destroyed, could she see her feelings in their true light.

She was physically attracted to Ellis, drawn helplessly by the same chemical reactions Martin found so fatal. This was the last monumental folly of all.

It took a strenuous effort to bring her attention back to Martin. She saw now that his lugubrious expression was faintly ridiculous. He was not built for high tragedy.

'Poor old Martin! Surely you needn't have swung the pendulum so far the other way – proposing to me, I mean?'

'Oh, I don't know.' He drained his glass and set it down. 'I knew we could be happy in a quiet way. Last night when you were so sure Ellis Ridley meant to have Angela, I decided to ask you. Selfish of me, in one way. I thought you'd help me to forget her. And I hoped you liked me enough to take a chance.

'There, that's the miserable truth,' he went on. 'I'm afraid I've made a hash of things all round. I knew all along Angela wanted Ridley, only I wouldn't face the truth. And *he's* the iron kind who never has any doubts.'

A flame of intense jealousy licked through her, searing all consciousness of Martin from her mind. 'The iron type who never has any doubts.' Yes, that was true. And Ellis would marry Angela.

And why not? Angela was out to please, her sights were set on Ellis and Peppercorn; while she herself had rejected his every attempt at kindness and consideration. Her mistaken loyalty to Douglas had blinded her to his virtues. Even his negligence concerning Douglas's accident was at that moment a less fault than his brother's unfaithfulness, a fault which a violent attraction could even bridge....

'I'm sorry, Grace.' Martin's voice roused her. 'Can you possibly just forget all this?'

'I don't see why not,' she smiled. 'And, Martin, the answer was no in any case. I wouldn't marry without love.'

'You mean the kind of love you had for Douglas Ridley?'

She sat playing with her gloves. 'That was a blind love. There's a better kind – a violent attraction if you like, but with it a love that recognizes faults and learns to accept them.' Her voice sank almost to a whisper. She was intensely moved by her own words, then immediately coldly despairing. It was too late, both for Martin and herself. Ellis and Angela would marry.

After a while she said: 'I see so many things clearly now. That time on the road, when we nearly collided with Ellis's car. You were so angry. It was jealousy, wasn't it? Not concern for me?'

'Yes. It was seeing them together—'

'And that night Ellis brought me home from Newcastle?'

'That night I'd been up to the Grange, you remember, attending the gardener's wife. I made the call an excuse to see Angela. She gave me a brutal brush-off, talked of no one but Ridley. I came home cut to ribbons by jealousy. Then Ridley arrived with you, and for one crazy moment I began to hope he had fallen for you. Then you more or less ran into my arms, relieved to be rid of him, and I knew I was wrong. I was beside myself with disappointment. That's why I spoke of him as I did.'

'How little any of us really know of each other,' Grace mused.

Martin reached over and patted her hand. 'I've tired you. And you've been more understanding than I deserve.'

'I think you've had a lucky escape, Martin. Angela isn't good enough for you.' She gathered up her wrap.

'But good enough for Ridley?'

Her face flamed. 'Not really.' She saw his surprise. 'Ellis is a bigger man than Douglas ever was.'

'You're not serious? I thought you—'

'He has his faults,' she said hastily, 'but I know

now I've been unfairly prejudiced against him. I've been proved wrong lately on too many points. . . . I think he's too good for Angela.'

Martin shrugged. 'If you say so. Anyway, as far as I'm concerned, you've come out of this situation with flying colours.'

'Have I?' He did not notice the tinge of sadness in her voice.

Two days passed, days of silent conflict for Grace. She found herself unwillingly tracing the past, fitting together the missing pieces. Now Douglas's treachery was established so many doubts became certainties, so many mysteries were solved.

It was a painful journey, but she forced herself to complete it. She looked once more through that album of photographs, that record of false happiness, then locked it away in a drawer. Released at last from loyalty to her dead she found a new clarity of mind. No longer a pale shadow of Douglas, she was free to live again.

And living now meant this powerful longing for Ellis. In one sense it had come with the impact of a thunderbolt; in another she recognized that it had been there all along, though disguised. With it came a new despair. Ellis was not for her. Even if he had not been almost engaged to Angela, her own pride would never allow her to reveal her feelings. Ellis was still guilty concerning Douglas's death. The old barrier still stood between them. She had accused him so often and the reason for those accusations still existed. Nothing had changed, she realized, except for this new raging ache for his presence, so powerful she was helpless before it.

It was a relief to be busy, to be hourly coping with

the demanding situation at Lintlaw House. Almost out of convalescence, Simon was daily regaining his tough and buoyant health. The school holidays were almost due, when Archie Scott would be free to play with him, but meanwhile he was restless and bored without the company of other children.

The weather had grown warm and humid. Heavy clouds massed above the rim of the vale, menacing with a promise of storm, but without breaking. Thick white mists veiled the mornings and gathered again at sunset. It was restless weather for a small boy with a vivid imagination.

Grace varied his days with walks, an occasional picnic and games in the garden, but there were still the household duties and the demands of Alec's practice. For some periods of the day Simon must amuse himself.

Thursday evening surgery saw Martin on duty. Alec was visiting his wife. For the first ten minutes there were no patients. Martin was chuckling over a handbill left in the waiting-room, concerning a Terrier Show and Fair to be held in the village early in August.

'Terrier Racing,' he read, 'Horn-Blowing and Halloaing – think I'd be any good at that, Grace? ... Shepherds' Crooks, Walking Sticks Plain and Fancy, Drinking a Yard of Ale – now that really does appeal. ... Sheaf-Tossing.... It's incredible. You're sure you don't dance round the maypole, too?'

'In August? Don't be daft! And I'll have you know they're all normal Show activities. Just routine.'

'Sounds pretty fantastic to me—'

They were interrupted by the sound of bustle and alarm from the waiting-room. Whipping open the connecting door, Grace found a man and woman supporting an elderly farmer in obvious pain. Calling Martin, she hurried forward to help.

'What's the trouble, Mrs. Cox?' she asked the woman, but it was the patient who answered. 'It's nowt, I tell ye. Something I've eaten—'

'He's been that sick, Doctor! I wanted to get the ambulance, but he wouldn't hear—'

'Right, let's have him on the couch!'

There was no difficulty about diagnosis. The signs were only too clear; the severe vomiting, distended abdomen, and quick, weak pulse. 'Peritonitis – get on the line for an ambulance,' Martin ordered.

The sudden emergency made heavy demands on them both. The patient collapsed after examination, and Grace had not only to attend him but try to comfort the frantic wife. The waiting room meanwhile was filling up, and by the time the ambulance had come and gone and normal order was restored, surgery was running a full half hour late.

As Martin pressed his bell for the last patient Grace slipped out to check on Simon. She had left him playing with his fort in the living-room, but for over an hour had been under too much stress to give him more than the odd thought. It was the time of day when he was used to playing alone, especially on surgery nights. She felt no anxiety when she discovered the room empty and the fort packed away. He must be in the garden or upstairs with his books.

She heard the surgery telephone ring as she went upstairs. By the time she had satisfied herself Simon was neither on the first nor the attic floor she heard Martin's car leave the drive. Downstairs again she looked in the surgery, found the call entered in the book, a farm near Glanton. Martin would be late for supper.

She ran into the garden, calling Simon's name, now just a shade worried. No answer came. She searched the garden methodically, looked in the old stables and the barn. He was nowhere to be seen, which meant he was probably somewhere across the fields. Clicking her tongue in vexation, she called again and again from the back boundary hedge. The mist was creeping up the fields, the clouds brooded ominously above the dark crags at the vale head. There was no sign of Simon's bright blue jersey in the wet, sloping fields. The sheep grazed in unconcern, turning mild, staring eyes at the sound of her voice.

Slipping through a back gate, she made a detour and came out on the road above the village. A local shepherd was just closing a field gate opposite, his collie at his heels. He gave Grace a nod. 'Was that you calling, Miss Haydon?'

'Yes. You haven't seen the doctor's little boy, have you?'

'Aye, I have. Over the brow yonder, walking up the road. I shouted at him, tell't him he'd best gan back, for there's a rare storm on the way. He said summat I couldn't catch – sounded like summat aboot a goat. But I had to get over to a sick ewe, so I thought no more on it.'

'A – goat?' Grace stood transfixed. The wild goats again! What else could take Simon in the direction of the hills? He couldn't have gone far, of course. But she cast a worried glance at the sky. Beneath the banked layers of elephant-coloured cloud it was now a lurid copper.

'How long ago was this?' she asked.

'More than half an hour, Miss Haydon, almost the three-quarters. He'll have been gone a canny time now.'

'Thanks, anyway. I'll get the car out.'

'Aye, ye'll soon pick him up. Good-night.'

He stumped away. It was then Grace remembered she had no car. Both Alec's and Martin's were out. A wave of anxiety almost swamped her. It was not that she was afraid of Simon getting lost. He had a good bump of locality. But to get a thorough soaking in the downpour which was almost certainly coming, this was the last thing she wanted to happen. It could even mean a serious setback in his health, if not worse. . . .

She pulled herself together. She could almost certainly beg a lift from some local person going that way. The idea of Goatshiels as Simon's destination became fixed in her mind. There had been all the talk of Goatshiels with old Will. And it had been on the last occasion, when old Will spoke of goats at Thrunton, that Simon had wandered that way.

Then she remembered something else. Until either Alec or Martin returned there was no one manning the telephone. On impulse she ran down to the Everitts' cottage and asked for Peggy. The girl was home and readily agreed to sit in the house and take any messages. When Grace saw her installed she ran out to the road again, signalled down the first car she saw coming. It pulled up.

'Want a lift? Oh, it's you, Grace!'

Angela's face appeared at the window of the elegant white saloon. Her cool beautiful eyes took in every detail of Grace's flushed dishevelment, the surgery overall open above a workaday sweater and skirt.

'Are you going to Peppercorn?' Grace stammered.

'Yes – why?'

In a few words she explained. Angela leaned across and opened the door. 'Better get in, then. He can't be far, surely, unless he begged a lift.'

'I didn't think of that,' said Grace, dismayed again.

'Well, if he's on the road we'll soon find him.' Angela let in the clutch, said contemptuously, 'Why don't you relax? If you ask me that brat needs a good spanking, anyway.'

'He *is* my responsibility.' Grace's gaze was raking the road ahead.

'You did take it on voluntarily, though, didn't you? And my guess is you're sick of the job already.'

'That's just not true. I'd do anything for Alec and Isobel.'

Angela was silent, driving now at a reckless speed on the almost empty road. Eventually Grace said: 'Three miles now, and no sign of him. He couldn't have walked so far without a lift. It looks as if you might be right—'

As they topped the brow of a hill they drove straight into the sagging cloud ceiling. Huge splashes of rain hit the windscreen, a gust of wind rocked the car. In minutes they were driving through a deluge.

'He won't be on the road in this!' Angela had to shout to make herself heard. 'He'll either be sheltering somewhere or getting a lift. I'm going to press on to Peppercorn. What do you want to do?'

'I'll come with you.' It seemed the best of half a dozen doubtful decisions.

Angela concentrated on her driving. Visibility was bad. Luckily there was little else on the road – a cattle-transporter rattling back to Abbotshaws, the local bus lumbering cautiously, a drenched motor-cyclist grimly riding the storm.

The road was awash at every declivity, the roadside firs swooped and bowed under the force of wind and water. Still Grace craned for a sight of Simon, longing yet dreading to see a woebegone little figure crouching in the dyke.

They were out of the vale now, climbing along Rylestone Edge, the shoulders of the hills giving welcome protection. The wet road, gleaming blue in the lurid light, looped emptily ahead. She relaxed a little. No one giving him a lift would set him down on this bleak expanse, where even the sheep holdings were miles apart.

Angela turned the car up the pass leading to Peppercorn. At the division of the tracks, a few miles further on, Grace's anxious eyes spied an object in the heather.

'Stop, please!' she begged. As Angela complied she was already half out of the car. She ran to pick up the school cap, dirty and sodden. Simon's name was inside. With a sinking heart she looked up the lonely track to Goatshiels. Low driving clouds obliterated the summits. A roll of thunder echoed in the distance.

'Is it Simon's?' Angela called.

Grace nodded. 'He must have got a lift, after all. He's gone to the High Stones now.'

Angela shrugged. 'Not a chance – in this! He'll have made a run for Peppercorn. Better come with me.'

Her voice was bored, unwelcoming.

'No. You don't know Simon.' Grace hesitated. Useless to explain about the wild goats. Angela would be incredulous. 'He could have got as far as this before the rain, with a lift. I think he'll be up at the High Stones.'

'You're not going up there – in this?'

'I've got to. Tell Ellis Ridley, will you? I might need help—'

Her voice dwindled before Angela's resigned stare. 'Oh, I'll tell him. But he'll only think as I do, that you're raving. And the kid's bound to be up at the house anyway.'

Grace was already drenched through her thin nylon overall. Angela threw an old raincoat from the back of the car. 'Here's a scarf, too, for your head.' Her tone was contemptuous. 'You must be out of your mind. And Ellis won't thank you if he has to turn out to find you. That mist's getting thicker every minute.'

'I'm not asking him to help me – only Simon, if need be.'

She donned the raincoat and scarf, turned her back on Angela and began plodding up the lonely track. She heard the car begin the long grinding climb to Peppercorn, and soon even that sound had gone, blanketed in mist.

Twilight gathered about her as she climbed. The rain eased now, but the mist thickened alarmingly as she climbed into the clouds. At last she was brought to a groping standstill, a prisoner in a smother of vapour, with no visibility beyond the heaped boulders at the path edge.

Fear settled on her, not for herself but Simon. Was he marooned as she was and afraid to move? Or was Angela right? Had he changed his mind at the ominous weather and turned up to Peppercorn?

She called his name over and over, hearing the echo flung back from rock faces, trapped in narrow gullies. She strained to hear beyond the echo, but there came only the occasional cry of a wandering sheep.

What should she do? Press on and risk being lost altogether and thus no use to Simon, or go back to Peppercorn?

It seemed wisest, after all, to retrace her steps. There was still that fifty-fifty chance Simon might be at the house; failing that surely she could call on Ellis's help, Angela or no Angela?

As she hurried back down the track she realized her own plight. Her thin surgery shoes and nyloned legs were saturated. She felt a chill in her very bones. Time enough, though, to worry over herself when Simon was safe.

She reached the division of the tracks and plunged upwards again towards Peppercorn. The sound of a car driven at speed drew her into the verge. Next moment Angela's white saloon loomed bouncing down the rough surface. It drew up beyond her with a squeal of tyres. Grace ran back.

Angela's face was white and vindictive. In reply to Grace's breathless question she snapped:

'I don't know if he's there or not. And I couldn't care less—'

'Didn't you ask Ellis—'

'No, I didn't! He wouldn't have been interested.' Angela's voice was a shaken rasp. Grace saw now that she was almost in a state of hysteria. 'He's too busy entertaining a friend – a very old friend. Why don't you go up and see for yourself?'

'But, Angela, I—'

Angela's face quivered. Angry tears shone in her eyes. 'Damn you, I tell you I don't know! And I wasn't likely to stay after what *I* saw . . . I've told you, if you don't believe me go see for yourself!'

The car shot forward again. Grace watched its

bumping descent, dazed by Angela's words.

'He isn't interested ... a very old friend—'

What was happening at Peppercorn? She dreaded the discovery awaiting her. Ellis must have some woman up there. Was he reverting to form again?

She mastered her repugnance, the rush of emotions that came unbidden. Simon was the one who mattered now.

She plodded upwards, reached the stableyard gate. The house itself was scarcely visible, its head in the cloud. She went through the shrubbery to the front garden. Light streamed from the uncurtained window. Grace heard loud strident music.

Now the interior of the room was revealed to her, significant as a lighted stage. With painful vividness she saw Ellis, lounging in an armchair, watching a small slender girl with hair like a flame, wearing a scanty green dress and swaying rhythmically to the music.

This then, was Wyn Everitt, once Douglas's girl. And now Ellis was dallying with her, an Ellis so treacherous that even Angela could not hold him from other women. Wyn's uninhibited laughter rang out, and at the sound Grace knew a blind angry despair, strong enough for a moment to blot out her anxiety for Simon.

And this too was history repeating itself. Here she was coming to Ellis Ridley for aid, as once Sandy Currie the shepherd had come. Now it was not Douglas lying at the foot of the High Stones – but it could be Simon. ...

Was Ellis Ridley to be once more 'not at home' when his help was urgently needed?

Wyn spun to a standstill, huddled gracefully on

the hearth. Ellis got up to pour drinks, a sardonic amusement on his face. Grace shrank away from the window, shrank too from the need to interrupt that intimate scene, but she had no choice.

Suddenly she was lifted by a wave of anger so fierce it brought a new strength and purpose. This time he *would* hear! This time his dalliance would be interrupted. Whatever his anger, his reluctance, he must be forced to listen, to act, to become for a few short hours the man she had thought him only days ago.

She ran to the great door and plied the knocker with all the force she could muster. The thunderous assault woke echoes throughout the house. She was still knocking when the door was torn open. Ellis Ridley was silhouetted against the light.

'What the devil!' he shouted. Then, on a note of amazement: 'Grace, what is it? What are you doing here?'

'Let me in,' she panted. 'I need help. It's Simon – he's lost on the High Stones . . . I'm sorry if I'm interrupting anything—' she flung the words like an insult – 'but you've got to help me!'

His hand closed over her arm and he jerked her indoors, eyeing her with a measured intimidation. His gaze slipped to her soaked clothes, her ruined shoes. He hustled her roughly into the living-room, thrust her with force into a chair. 'Now, what's all this? Simon, you say? That child – at the High Stones on a night like this?'

'That's what I'm trying to tell you – he must have got a lift – he's still looking for wild goats: . . . I know it sounds mad, but it's true. We've got to get up there – he may be hurt, lost in the mist—' Her voice cracked in terror. 'Help me – help me, please.'

She found the rim of a glass at her lips. 'Drink!' he ordered. She swallowed raw burning spirit. It galloped like fire through her veins, cut through her hysteria, stilled her trembling. She opened her eyes, saw Wyn Everitt watching her with frightened eyes.

'Ellis, what's wrong? Who is she—'

'Never mind, Wyn!' he cut in ruthlessly. 'It's an emergency.' He grasped Grace's shoulder. 'What about Doctor Haydon – where is he?'

'At Newcastle, and Martin's out on call. There's no one—'

'What time does your brother get back?'

'About half-past nine. Sometimes earlier.'

'Right!' He swung to face Wyn. 'You'd better get down there, wait for Doctor Haydon at the surgery, tell him what's happened—'

'You mean tell him—'

'Tell him his son is lost on Goatshiels and that we've gone to find him. He'd better get up here as quickly as he can. Go on now, there's a good girl.'

'You mean – this is Grace Haydon?' There was guilt and embarrassment in her face now.

'Yes, but never mind that now, girl!' he roared. 'Get in your car and on your way. And take care how you drive.'

'I'll be all right, Ellis.' She whipped up her coat from a chair and was gone.

'Now, Grace—' Ellis turned to her. 'I'll be getting my car out while you find your breath again. And get out of those rubbishy shoes. You'll find an assortment of rubber boots in the conservatory. Meet me in the yard!'

His rapped directions jerked her to action. She found the boots, stripped off her raincoat and huddled into an ancient duffle from the pegs. In the stable-yard Ellis's tall figure moved about in a stream of light from the garage, casting a black fantastic shadow.

'Ready? In you get, then.'

He flung himself before the wheel, steered the car through the gate and began the descent, the fog lamp piercing the layers of mist ahead.

'Now, tell me what happened,' he commanded. 'Tell me how the devil he gave you the slip this time. Or were you too busy dallying with Doctor Finch?'

'Now dare you!' she flared. '*You* – after the way you—'

'Never mind that now, whatever it means. How did Simon get so far before you took alarm?'

'There was an emergency at the surgery. We were up to our eyes. . . . Oh, what does it *matter*?' she flung at him. Why should she seek to justify herself in his eyes? Never now could he justify himself in hers. Only one thing had surprised her, his instant reaction to the requirements of the situation.

She gave up the struggle to reconcile her warring emotions. Her recent acceptance of the fact that she loved him had done battle against the swooping disillusion of that scene with Wynne, against all the rioting questions that scene brought. This confused locking of truths and half-truths, of attraction and repulsion, she must erase from her mind.

This man, she reminded herself, was her only hope where Simon was concerned. Everything else could wait.

'This was where I found his cap. I didn't get much further. The mist closed in—'

He nodded, spurring the car up the Goatshiels track.

Gradually it closed in until it almost disappeared. He stopped the car, shut off the engine. 'This is as far as we can go – on wheels.' They got out, stood in a listening attitude. It was almost dark. They heard muffled sheep calls, the harsh croak of a crow.

Ellis called Simon's name, the echo reverberating among the rocks; called and listened, called and listened again. 'Can you hear anything?' he demanded.

'No.'

He ferreted in the car for a large torch, then switched off the headlights. From the boot he drew a stout coil of rope.

'I'm going to take the track along the top of the High Stones. You'd better stay in the car.'

'I'm coming too. If he's hurt or fallen down somewhere, it'll take two of us – you know that,' she protested.

'Have you ever walked this path?'

'By daylight, yes.'

'You know it's like a razor's edge in parts? That it's damned dangerous?'

'I'm still coming.'

He hesitated. 'Right, I'll go first. Follow exactly where I tread – understand? If you see or hear anything stop me.'

He passed one end of rope round her waist, made a careful knot, took it several turns round his own body and slung the spare coil over his shoulder. 'Don't worry,' he said caustically, 'I shan't slip and pull you down. I'm an experienced rock climber. On the other hand if you slip I'll be able to haul you back. Right?'

She nodded. He flashed his torch on the beginning of the grassy sheep track. Together they began the dark perilous journey along the brink of the High Stones.

CHAPTER EIGHT

SHE remembered the path well, but when she had climbed it with Douglas it had been on a winsome September day, the turf bright with harebells and fading ling, the white flash of the curlews above. She knew that in places the ridge narrowed to less than the height of a man, that there were broken fissures, buttresses of piled boulders half blocking the track. Even in daylight it had taken nimble feet and a watchful eye.

Now she was walking it in the blanketing mist-thickened darkness, seeing in the torchlight a pair of man's heels before her, set deliberately along the deviating path, now lifted to climb a rocky shelf, now slithering into an earthy hollow. And after his feet she set her own, a heart-stopping journey of sudden drops and climbs which ended blindly in mist and more mist, a stifling curtain which could hide a murderous drop to the razor-edged slabs of rock far below.

Every so often Ellis halted, called Simon's name in a forceful voice echoing from crag to crag. Still no response but the flurried screech of a startled bird. Then on again.

There came a moment when Ellis lifted his foot from a thin slab of rock. Grace set her own foot on it, only to feel it lurch and slide. The balance of her body was violently shifted. She was thrown at an angle, her feet beginning a helpless slither along with the stone. As it tilted into nothingness a scream broke from her. Then every muscle in her body was jarred as his hand bit like a clamp round her arm and she was hoisted upright again.

He held her close to steady her, and she could hear his heart drumming against her own, struggled against a whirling faintness.

'It's all right, Grace, I've got you.' He shone his torch downwards. Where they stood a cleft in the path had been naturally bridged by sandwiched layers of slabs. They heard a cacophony of crashes as the fallen stone fell from ridge to ridge of the rock face below. She shuddered. 'Can we go on? Is there anywhere to walk?'

'Yes, it's wider just ahead. Can you make it?'

She nodded, somehow finding the strength to force her shaking body in his wake. The nearness of the fall had served to demonstrate the urgent need to press on. Simon, too, could have made such a slip.

The thought chilled her. Again Ellis halted and called. Again there was no reply.

'A patch of bog here,' he said presently. 'We'll have to jump it.' She saw him spring, slither and then right himself. His hands reached out to her across the mist. 'Jump – I'll catch you!'

She sprang blindly, her hands meeting his. Again she felt herself clamped in an iron hold. They paused for breath. Ellis called again. As the echoes died away Grace clutched at his arm. 'Listen – I heard something. Call again!'

'Simon, where are you?' Eerily the echo wailed in reply. Then this time he heard it too, a faint shivering cry which seemed to come from ahead but below the level of their feet.

'Oh, thank God!' Tears of relief rushed to her eyes.

'He's conscious, anyway,' Ellis said grimly. 'But we

won't congratulate ourselves yet.'

They continued in agonizing slowness, calling repeatedly, at last Ellis halted again. Simon's voice sounded immediately below. They edged towards the rim and called again.

'I've hurt my foot – I can't get up!' came a faint little voice.

'Hold on, darling. It's Auntie Grace and Mr. Ridley. We'll get you!' She turned to Ellis, waiting for a lead. Her trust in him as a rescuer was absolute.

He shone his torch over the lip of the crag, swung the ray this way and that. 'I see him. He's on a ledge about twelve feet down – lying pretty near the edge too.' He cupped his hands about his mouth. 'Simon, this is Ellis Ridley. Now listen to me. I'm coming down. But you mustn't try to move or watch me. Understand – just lie perfectly still.'

'I'll try, Mr. Ridley.' Grace heard the terrified sob bitten gamely back.

Ellis turned to Grace. 'I'm going down to put the rope on him, but I can't just haul him up the rock face. He's too hurt and shocked to help himself. I need you to guide him up. Have you the guts to go down there?'

'Yes,' she said faintly. 'Anything – for Simon.'

'Good for you!' He slipped the rope from his shoulders, tested the knot at her waist. 'You'll have to go first. I can climb down there without a rope—'

'You can't!' she gasped. 'You might fall—'

'I won't fall. Stop arguing. Got a good head for heights?' he shot at her.

'Not really, but that doesn't matter.' Yet fear had settled on her like a clammy hand.

'You can't fall.' His voice was terse. He was already anchoring his feet behind a slab of rock. 'You know that nothing in heaven or hell would make me let go – *don't you?*'

'Yes, Ellis.'

She crawled to the edge, knew a moment of black annihilating panic, then lowered herself over. Fear of failing under those watchful eyes was greater at that moment than her fear of heights. It was a tense, sweating eternity before she felt the rope tauten, then gradually, clinging to clefts in the rock face, she lowered herself to the ledge.

Her first action was to ease Simon's small body back from the lip. The ledge itself was no more than four feet wide and only the fact that it was canted at an angle had saved Simon from a further fall. Simon moaned. 'Is that you, Auntie Grace? I hoped you would come. My foot hurts – that's how I couldn't get up.'

'I know. Don't try to talk.'

Ellis called: 'I'm coming down, Grace.' He made a sure and skilful descent. She had already untied the rope and now he knelt to fasten it round Simon. 'You'll have to be a good soldier, Simon. I'm going to haul you up, and your aunt will help you from below. Try to grin and bear it, won't you?'

'Yes, Mr. Ridley.'

The operation took time, skill and considerable effort. Grace supported Simon as far as she could, but there came one cold, empty moment when he swung in mid-air. Ellis leaned out at a perilous angle and grabbed him, pulling him gently to safety. Finally Grace roped herself and climbed again up the jutting shelves of rock to his strong waiting hands.

After a short pause for breath they turned to Simon.

Ellis directed the torch while Grace took the injured foot gently in her hands. Simon yelped as she slipped off his wellington boot. 'I'll try not to hurt you, darling. Is it your ankle?'

'Ouch, yes! When I slipped over the edge I fell right on it.'

'A bad sprain, I think. I'm certain it's not broken. And he's probably badly bruised too.' She looked up at Ellis. 'Can we get him back – along there?'

He shook his head. 'Be madness to try. I've got another idea. There's an old shepherd's hut further on where the ridge widens. It's just under the lee of the crag on the south side. We can shelter there until the mist clears, or wait for first light. Will you stay with him while I take the torch and reconnoitre?'

'You won't – lose us?' Her voice shook. She needed him. The flag of her pride was at the foot of the mast now. His strength, his authority, his resourcefulness were their only hope.

'I won't lose you, Grace,' he said quietly, and was gone. She watched the light of his torch until it was just a brighter patch of the mist itself, then it was gone altogether.

Simon groped for her hand, said fretfully: 'Are you angry, Auntie Grace?'

'Not now. How did you get here?'

'I got a lift in a van. I didn't know it was going to rain then. A shepherd said something about a storm, but I thought he was joking. You were so busy in the surgery. I thought I'd just have a look for the wild goats ... I didn't know it was so far to the High Stones. ...'

'Never mind now.'

'There weren't any goats, Auntie Grace. Old Will

says you've got to have faith if you want to see things. Well, I *had*. But they weren't there, just a few old sheep. Then the mist came—'

'Don't try to talk. Cuddle up against me – you'll keep warm then.' She saw with relief that he was wearing his duffle coat.

It seemed a long time before the mist brightened ahead, became suffused with torchlight. A great thankfulness eased her. She heard Ellis's voice.

'I've found it. Here, let me have him. It's pretty safe going. Just follow on as you did before.'

A little over ten minutes of careful progress brought them to a down-sloping path. They reached the rough stone hut, and next moment were all inside, the door shut against the mist and the dark.

Ellis propped the torch on the window ledge and gently lowered Simon to a rough bench in the corner. 'There you are, son.' He stripped off his raincoat and covered the child, the warm tartan lining against him. 'One thing we can have, and that's a fire. There's always a good stock of wood left here.'

Grace saw a primitive stone fireplace, hewn logs heaped at the side. Ellis twisted newspapers from a heap in the corner, piled on first small, then larger logs, and started a blaze.

'There, that looks more like home. Now, the next essential.' He drew a brandy flask from his pocket, persuaded Simon to take a wry mouthful, then passed it to her.

'Go on, drink a good wallop. You'll need it to offset the chill you've probably got.'

Ten minutes later the fire was giving off a comforting heat. Simon had slipped into an exhausted doze and Grace, perched on the bench edge, felt the brandy heat in her veins slowly diffusing through her body.

Ellis lit a cigarette. His eyes met hers in an expressionless stare. 'It'll be a long night. I advise you to take off that duffle coat, lie down with the boy and cover yourself with it. You'll probably sleep.'

'What about you?'

'I'll stay awake a while.' He perched himself on an old box and folded his arms.

Grace lay down as directed, hugging Simon for warmth, but instead of sleep came welling, aching tears. The night stretched ahead, hours virtually alone with this man whom she loved and hated with such equal force. Behind her closed lids was a vivid picture of his seated, firelit figure.

After a while a low voice came: 'Why are you crying, Grace?'

She lay rigid, her heart racing. 'Don't pretend to be asleep,' he rasped. 'I'm not so easily deceived.'

She groped for her handkerchief, scrubbed her eyes and sat up. Ellis threw more logs on the blaze. She came to sit on the edge of the bench, opposite him across the hearth. His cool eyes appraised her.

'That's better, except that you look rather the worse for wear. And you needn't be ashamed of a few tears, *if* it's just shock reaction. But I've an idea it's rather more than that, isn't it?'

She gazed at him in silence. At that moment any explanation seemed impossible. The lost end of that tangled skein seemed irretrievable.

'Right, then! Let's go back to the moment you arrived at Peppercorn. You were angry. Am I right in supposing you resented my visitor?'

'I know who she is.'

'That didn't require much deduction.'

'I mean I know all about her.'

'I wonder if you do.' His eyes gleamed in challenge. 'What *do* you know?'

'That she was Douglas's girl – that he deceived me and met her here at the High Stones, after he was engaged to me. I found a letter among his things.'

'So you have no illusions left?'

She shook her head. 'No illusions – about either you or Douglas.'

His dark brows drew together. 'Well now, so that's the way it is?'

'That's the way it is.' She pushed back her damp, mist-spangled hair, then held her hands to the blaze. Her throat ached, the tears were near again. This turning over the ashes was hateful, yet held its own dark fascination.

'And you are convinced Wyn is now – my girl?' he pressed.

'When it suits you, I suppose.' Her tone quickened. 'When it's convenient to deceive Angela. You're just Douglas all over again. . . . That night he died, she was here then, wasn't she?'

'Go on!' His voice came taut and goading.

'Douglas waited for her at the High Stones. And meanwhile you – and she—!' She hesitated, then flung at him: 'That's why he died, because you weren't available to help him. It was double treachery. . . . And tonight again, I thought it would be history repeating itself—'

Her voice died. The flames dimmed and his face was lost in shadow. His voice cut in harshly: 'Truth may be stranger than fiction, but surely even you must see that the train of coincidences takes some swallowing. It's too pat altogether. But perhaps you prefer conjecture, half-truths, suppositions – heavily weighted, of course, by prejudice?'

She was silent, disturbed by his words.

'Prejudice,' he repeated. 'You want to hark back to the night of Douglas's death? Right. The pity is you didn't do it long ago. You've been bitterly incensed against me all along, Grace. The least you could have done, at the time it happened, was to ask me for my version—'

'You didn't offer it!'

'No, I didn't!' His voice rose, then remembering the sleeping child he dropped it again. 'I didn't explain or excuse myself because you in turn didn't trouble to ask me; because you accepted without verification the popular version that scandalized Abbotshaws and district!'

She flinched before his anger. 'I believed it, that's why.'

'You believed it, yes. You judged, tried and sentenced me without hearing my defence.'

She was shaken, knowing his words to be true. 'Yes, I did, but with good reason. No man who was innocent of negligence concerning his brother's death would accept such condemnation without defending himself.'

'So you gave a verdict of "Guilty"? And what if he had a sound reason for holding his tongue?'

He threw a couple of logs on the embers. A flame mounted, illumining his face, deepening the clefts by his mouth, throwing into stark relief the white scar at his temple.

'A sound reason?' she faltered.

'Oh yes. No man likes to be unpopular, to be the

object of busy scandal, to see other men turn their backs on him at auctions and horse shows. All that happened to me, Grace, until the nine days' wonder was over. Happily, most people easily forget – and forgive.' His last words were laced with sarcasm.

'I'm here now,' she said. 'I can't get away, even if I wanted to. I'm ready to listen to what you have to say.'

'Even if it disposes of your last illusions about Douglas?'

'Yes.'

He offered her a cigarette. She took it, feeling the need of a smoke screen. The deep, biting challenge of his eyes was too disconcerting without.

'We'll go back a long way, then – back to this.' He touched his scar. 'How do you think I got it?'

'A filly kicked you – or so Douglas said. You'd been cruel to her.'

A bitter smile curved his mouth. 'The truth was it was Douglas who ill-treated her. When she lashed out I happened to be in the way, stooping to pick up the leading rein. Douglas had the good fortune to possess a mother who was congenitally incapable of doubting her son's word. I had the misfortune to have a father whose wife could persuade him day was night and black was white. The filly was taken from me for my supposed behaviour, and *I* was marked for life.'

He flicked his ash in the flames. 'I tell you this, not out of any self-pity, but just to get the record straight. Douglas was a born liar, a born opportunist. He had all his mother's fatal charm, a gift which made him irresistible to women, as you yourself discovered. He was jealous of me because I was the eldest, because

Peppercorn was intended for me. But eventually my stepmother persuaded Father to make over a half-share to Douglas. Only this unsatisfactory arrangement has ever accounted for the fact that Douglas and I lived together. Neither of us would part with our share or our rights. It has been a house divided against itself.'

He was silent a moment, then continued: 'I prefer not to remember the years of my boyhood. The loss of my own mother made me difficult, stirred up a hell's brew of psychiatric problems. Oh, I was no angel! As soon as school was behind me I escaped from family life. It took several foreign trips and adventures galore before I found my real self and drove the old bitterness from my heart. And women helped – bold, bad and generous. Women you would probably despise, but who gave me back my confidence and my manhood.'

He threw his cigarette end in the fire. 'Enough of the background. Now, about the night of Douglas's death. As you know, he was deceiving you. Wyn Everitt, bless her, was an old flame of his. You may well ask – *and mine*? I see it in your face. But we'll come to that later. Wyn was in love with him before he attached himself to you. And I think he loved her in his own way, until you came along. He wanted you, but knew he could only get you through marriage. Conveniently enough, Wyn went over to Rothbury to work, and for a time he was able to keep her at arm's length – *until* she learned he was engaged to you. Wyn had fire and guts. She believed Douglas owed her marriage and began to show her hand in no mean way. Douglas met her at odd times and in desolate places, with a view to keeping her quiet. I first found out about these meetings on the night of his death.'

'Only then?'

'Only then. I met Wyn at the division of the tracks. I was coming back in the car from High Haugh. To see her there, just turning up the Goatshiels track into thick mist – naturally enough I was puzzled and questioned her. She told me what was afoot. I think she was too upset to care about secrecy any longer. I persuaded her to come back to the house and talk it over, for two reasons. One, I was concerned about your future happiness. Two, I considered she was walking into actual physical danger, broaching the High Stones path in such weather.'

Grace sat absorbed in his story, scarcely breathing. He continued: 'One thing about Wyn, she had always listened to me, accepted my advice. I told her just what I thought of her – and Douglas. I warned her that he would never marry her, that he considered her beneath him. I also challenged her sense of pride and independence. Wyn *is* a proud girl. Her family have been shepherds in this district for generations. She has an innate sense of natural dignity, and only her fatal obsession for Douglas could have reduced her to such humiliating tactics.'

'And she – listened to you?'

'Oh yes. She did more. She angrily rejected Douglas there and then – determined to have it out with him once and for all that very night. I had to go away that evening, to stay overnight in Newcastle. I left her in the house waiting for Douglas to come back. The mist had thickened even more. It took me all my time to grope my way in the car down to Rylestone Edge, where it lifted a little.'

He held her eyes, driving his point home. 'You understand – I was *not* at home when Sandy came for help. Only Wyn was there, playing the radiogram to while away the time. She heard nothing, but then Wyn likes her music loud and clear, as you no doubt noticed tonight. In the end Sandy gave up and went over to Lordhope instead, as you know. And the delay was fatal.'

'So you weren't anywhere near Peppercorn?' The weight of the truth dazed her.

'No, by that time I had probably reached Rothbury.'

'But why – why didn't you tell me all this?'

'One reason you already know,' he said coolly. 'Because you evidently liked and accepted the popular version. The other reason? I couldn't tell the truth without shattering your illusions about Douglas. And make no mistake – I had been tempted many times to do that already, when he was alive. But dead – no. You had already lost him and I saw just what it did to you. I couldn't take it on myself to complete the damage.'

She was trembling now. 'Any other man would—'

'I doubt it. You were the epitome of the maiden in distress, the fairy in mourning. At the funeral you looked so fragile – like the last flickering flame of a candle. A breath might have blown you out. And my back was broad. I had sweated out many worse situations as a boy. If anyone had to suffer I preferred it to be me.'

'And – Wyn? She agreed to keep quiet?'

'Yes. She was only too relieved to escape the scandal. Remember she had a job to keep, a family to placate.'

She nodded. Her mind was dazed and troubled.

The enormity of the truth lay heavily on her. And yet how simple it all was, after all....

'Thank you for telling me. But I wish now you *had* told me the truth at the time,' she ventured.

'You wish it now – yes. But the truth might have destroyed you then.'

Again great forces swayed her mind. This, then, was Ellis, the real Ellis; the man who had shouldered scorn and ignominy to save her distress. She remembered with grief the long months of false condemnation, the fixed haunting prejudice. She remembered her mourning for a worthless man, the wasted days of her London exile....

Ellis was smoking again, his face set in sombre lines, his gaze on the embers. Her pride was in the dust now, but his was inviolate as ever. He had never looked more unapproachable.

She began shakily. 'I misjudged you, Ellis. I did you a great wrong. I've been blind, too. Now you've explained it all I can't understand why I didn't guess – especially when I began to find out about Douglas.'

'Oh, I played the part well. Then gradually I began to hope I might wipe out the past, win your regard in other ways. I tried to be around when you needed me—' He broke off. 'But you're still wondering why Wyn was here tonight. And for that matter where Angela comes into it.'

'Yes, I am.'

'Wyn came tonight because I invited her. I wanted to talk to her and could scarcely visit her at her mother's house without undue curiosity from her family. Granted you saw what looked like a tempting situation. Wyn had been amusing herself playing records while I was involved with a long phone call.

I'd just come back into the room when you arrived, and by that time Wyn had agreed to do as I asked.'

'And what was that?'

'To tell you exactly what happened the night Douglas died.' He drew on his cigarette, blew smoke deliberately. Only now he avoided her eyes.

'Why, Ellis?' Her heart slipped into a hurried beat. She felt herself on the verge of a big discovery.

He turned to face her. 'Because a man can take only so much of loss and heartache; because whatever I did or tried to do for you Douglas's death was still between us,' he raged. 'It was there like the Berlin wall, unscalable. And the irony of it became too much for me. Douglas dead – you unattached again. Yet I'd built that wall in blood and sweat, with my own two hands. I'd made such a damned good job of it I'd eternally separated us. And just suddenly – not being a story-book hero – I couldn't take any more, Grace. Call it weakness, call it what you like, but I had to demolish that wall. I had to meet you again on open ground, as a man who owed you nothing, a man who would willingly do anything for you but live a lie any longer!'

The force and passion of his words stirred her unbearably. She stood up, a hand to her throat. 'Ellis—' she whispered.

He rose and reached for her. He held her hands and looked down into her eyes. And in those grey depths she saw a raw, intolerable pain break and recede, saw in its place a dawning wonder and joy.

'I love you,' he said softly. 'I've loved you from the moment you walked into that party of yours – the night I called you a Brinkburn fairy. All right, so I squired Angela around. Don't ask me why – I couldn't tell you. Habit, perhaps, the need to salvage my pride, pretend I was heart-whole. I wasn't in love with her, never have been. And I've given her no reason to think so. It was you all the time, Grace—'

She hid her face against him. 'If only I'd known! It's been such a struggle, loving you and trying to fight it because of Douglas—'

He tipped up her chin. 'So I didn't imagine it?' His eyes were bemused. 'It was there all the time, that fascination between us. You felt it too. . . . No, don't talk – not now.'

He folded her in his arms, kissed her with a passion and emotion never reached by Douglas. She clung to him, drowning in fierce joy. And, as if at some hidden signal, at that moment the light of the torch flickered and died, leaving them together in deep shadow.

They talked for several hours before she eventually obeyed his suggestion that she lie down and rest. Happiness made nonsense of sleep. Her whirling mind allowed her only an hour of unconsciousness before she woke to the discomfort of aching bones, to the sight of faint misty sunshine at the small hut window. She sat up to see Ellis set wide the door. The damp, cool air rushed in. Simon stirred and yawned.

'Looks good, doesn't it?' Ellis smiled. 'And the sooner we're on our way the better.'

Some ten minutes later they left the hut, Ellis carrying Simon piggy-back, Grace walking behind along the ridge. Though the mist still lay thickly in the hollows and valleys, visibility was good enough to make nonsense of the night's dangers. They had reached the point where Grace had slipped on the piled shelves of rock when suddenly Ellis checked. He reached a warning hand behind him as if to silence her. Puzzled, she obeyed. Then:

'Look, Simon,' she heard him whisper. 'Over there – on that high rock... !'

She followed his gaze to a ridge some fifty yards ahead, the sun gilding its rim with gold. There, stark against the backdrop of pearly mist, stood a great grey and white goat, its down-curving horns like scimitars, its head rigid, watchful. The wild, noble creature might have been posing for a picture by Landseer. As they stood frozen, watching, the first of the sun's rays crept over the high southern ridge, gilded the wild goat in splendour, turned him into a fabled beast on an armorial shield. The sight was all at once too much for Simon. He shrieked: 'It's a wild goat – it is! Look, Auntie Grace! O-oh! He's gone—'

At the first sound of his voice the goat stiffened. His tail came up to flare along his spine. He lifted his head, stamped the ground, once, twice, then with a bound had disappeared down the slope beyond, into the thickest blanketings of the mist.

'It's like a miracle!' Grace gasped.

Simon's eyes brimmed with delight and wonder. 'It *is* a miracle, Auntie Grace. Old Will says they still happen, only you've got to have faith.'

Ellis said softly, his eyes meeting hers: 'Ah, but Goatshiels is a place of miracles, Simon.'

It was true, Grace told herself. Once it had been a place of death and haunting horror. Now she knew that all her life she would remember this moment of pure thrilling joy, the twin miracles of Simon's dream and her own happiness.

Three months later, in mild autumn weather, a

car climbed the track to Peppercorn. The honeymoon in France was over. Ellis and Grace were coming home.

Lovingly Grace's eyes dwelt on each turn of the track. The hills cast deep shadows as the sun dwindled down the sky. Signs of winter were about in the russet of the dying bracken, the dark withered stems of the heather. As always the white-faced Cheviots grazed on the verge. She was agitated by happiness, by the knowledge that at last she could call Peppercorn home.

So much had happened in the past few months. Their wedding had been the talk of the district. No one had been more surprised than Jess, nor in the end so loyally thankful. 'For he's found love at last,' she admitted. 'The love he's aye looked for and never found.'

Isobel was home and well again, taking her place in the household, though this time with the added help of Peggy Everitt, who had finally rebelled against Mrs. Forster's stingy treatment. Alec found a cure for Simon's wanderings in the welcome opening of a Scout and Cub group in the village. He enrolled his son as one of the first Cub members, knowing Simon would find all the adventure he needed under proper control.

Meanwhile Simon paid many visits to old Will, to recount over and over again his sight of the wild goat of Goatshiels.

The news of Grace's engagement had shocked Angela into leaving Abbotshaws for London, where she was making headway as a television announcer. Martin had gradually recovered from his obsession for her and was turning for company to quiet Helen Adams.

Wyn Everitt had written from Manchester to congratulate Grace. 'I hope the past is forgiven,' her letter ran. 'You more than anyone will understand how I came to fall for Douglas. Now I know you will be happy with Ellis. He will never let you down. . . .'

And now, as the chimneys of Peppercorn appeared, Ellis and Grace saw the smoke rising high in the still air, sign that Jess had kept a promise to open the house for them.

They mounted to the ridge above the burn, saw at last the house in full view, facing the wild waste of hills, in its own little acre of cultivation.

Grace quoted softly:

'Tell him to buy me an acre of land,
Parsley, Sage, Rosemary and Thyme.
And sow it all over with one Peppercorn—'

Ellis stopped the car and took her hand in his. His bronzed face was tender, the scar whitely prominent.

'Can't you finish it?' he teased.

'No, because it doesn't fit.' She smiled, added slowly: 'For *now* he is a true love of mine! Will that do?'

He held her gently and kissed her. Together they gazed at the lonely, moving sight of the house among the hills.

'Welcome home, darling,' he said.